NO CONTEST

Lady Drewe was accustomed to playing games of rough-and-tumble with her older brothers. But Lord GlenRoss was proving to be a different kind of adversary.

Easily, this powerful gentleman had gained the upper hand. As she squirmed in his iron grip, he said with a smile, "But I have been less than gentlemanly. A gentleman should always give in to a lady. And since you're in the mood for a quarrel, I'll give you even further provocation, if you wish."

He held her wrists immobile with one hand, and with his other took her head captive. Only slowly did it dawn on Drewe that his object was to kiss her . . . and that this was one test of strength she wanted to lose . . . .

DAWN LINDSEY was born and grew up in Oklahoma, where her ancestors were early pioneers, so she came by her fascination with history naturally. After graduating from college she pursued several careers, including writing romance novels.

The Barbarous Scot

by
Dawn Lindsey

Ⓢ
A SIGNET BOOK

SIGNET
Published by the Penguin Group
Penguin Books USA Inc., 375 Hudson Street,
New York, New York, 10014, U.S.A.
Penguin Books Ltd, 27 Wrights Lane, London W8 5TZ, England
Penguin Books Australia Ltd, Ringwood, Victoria, Australia
Penguin Books Canada Ltd, 10 Alcorn Avenue, Toronto, Ontario, Canada M4V 3B2
Penguin Books (N.Z.) Ltd, 182-190 Wairau Road,
Auckland 10, New Zealand

Penguin Books Ltd, Registered Offices:
Harmondsworth, Middlesex, England

First published by Signet, an imprint of New American Library,
a division of Penguin Books USA Inc.

First Printing, December, 1991

10 9 8 7 6 5 4 3 2 1

1

Lady Drewe Carlisle swept quickly through the crowded ballroom, ignoring the many glances, not all of them admiring, that followed her tall figure. She looked to be in a rage, which was by no means unusual, since she was noted for her volatile temper. But at least it had the doubtful felicity of being extremely becoming to her, for her unusual amber eyes were sparkling with suppressed fury, and there was a lovely color in her beautiful stormy face, which too often tended to be merely bored or discontent.

But then, not even her worst detractors—and she had many—could deny that all the Carlisles were extremely handsome. Lady Drewe might shock the prudish with her language and her outrageous conduct, but she was undoubtedly a diamond of the first water. She might have chosen to deck herself that evening in a ball gown of amber silk guaranteed to raise the hackles of the disapproving, since it clung so faithfully to her admittedly excellent figure that a few of the more scandalized were ready to swear her petticoats had been damped. The fashion of discarding one's hoops and attiring oneself in public in what looked for all the world like a chemise had only recently been introduced from France, and few had yet dared to adopt it. But not even the most scandalized could deny that on her tall, graceful figure it was vastly becoming.

Her quarry at the moment seemed to be the younger of

her two brothers, which did surprise a few of the observers. All the Carlisles were notoriously wild to a fault, but the Honorable Charles was considered by many to be the most likable of the family.

He was a tall exquisite, dressed in the height of style, his evening dress boasting the exaggerated collar and lapels of the latest mode and an immense *boutonnière* of pink carnations. Like his sister, he was always among the first to adopt a new mode, so that his hair was worn in the new shorn style recently made fashionable on the Continent that was supposed to be reminiscent of ancient Rome. Most had by then given up elaborate wigs and powdering that had been fashionable for so long, especially after the iniquitous tax on powder had passed some five years before, but the number there that evening who still clung to bagwigs or their own hair tied at the neck was high; and in that company the Honorable Charles looked almost as startling as his sister did.

He was at the moment propped against a post, openly ogling a dashing brunette in silver spangles. He looked slightly uneasy at his sister's approach, and said plaintively before she could open her mouth, "If you're in a temper, m'dear, as you look to be, I should warn you I'm in no mood for a family scene tonight."

"Never mind that!" she said in her distinctive abrupt way, her eyes still flashing becomingly. "Where's Harry?"

"Dash it, I don't know, and what's more to the point, I don't want to know!" complained her brother indignantly, returning to his scrutiny of the ripe brunette. "Much more restful when Harry ain't around. You should know that by now. Quarrel with him later, if you must. Or better, yet, don't quarrel with him at all. You know it don't do the least good. Harry's a devil."

Lady Drewe gave an unamused laugh. "I'm afraid this quarrel won't wait. Where is he? In the card room?"

The brunette had unfortunately passed out of sight, so the Honorable Charles sighed and reluctantly brought his attention back to his sister. "What's he done now?" he inquired without much interest.

"He has even outdone himself, if one can believe the rumors—and I have no difficulty in doing so," Lady Drewe exclaimed scornfully. "At least four people tonight have taken immense pleasure in telling me that, not content with the scandal last month involving Bracton's wife, he must needs elope with some little *bourgeoisie.*"

"Lord, what's new in that?" protested Charlie. "Never hear of him but what he's involved with some female or another."

"The difference is, until now he has at least confined himself to the dubious virtue of seducing other men's wives! Worse, he bungled the whole thing, in his usual fashion, with the result that the girl's father discovered the flight in time to overtake them on the Bath road. There was a brawl—I can scarcely call it an affair of honor!" she said contemptuously, "and the father was seriously wounded. The girl is said to be in decline, the father on the brink of death, and our name once more bandied about on every vulgar tongue! Very pretty, isn't it?"

"Good God, what in the fiend's name possessed him to take her to Bath?" demanded the Honorable Charlie, ever one who liked to get to the heart of the matter. "Seems a damn fool thing to do, even for Harry. Nothing there but tabbies and Bath quizzes."

Lady Drewe hunched a beautiful shoulder, left bare by the extreme décolleté of her amber gown. "Is that all you have to say? I tell you, he has gone too far this time. As near as I can tell, he has debauched half the women in England already, but this—"

"I fear you flatter me, my dear," interrupted a drawling

voice from behind her. "Modesty forces me to admit it has been no more than a fourth."

Both brother and sister turned quickly to survey Viscount Graydon, rakishly handsome in evening dress, his habitual sneer very much in evidence.

None of the siblings were much alike, save that all were extraordinarily good-looking. Lord Graydon, the eldest, possessed the family's distinctive straight profile and tall grace, and his hair, less rigidly cropped than his younger brother's, was more dark than fair. He was undoubtedly handsome, but overlying all was an air of cynicism that was almost a sneer, which marred his natural good looks. He was profligate of habit, possessed an unsavory reputation with women, and was known to be extremely vicious when crossed.

The Honorable Charles, the next eldest, was fairer and less complicated. He possessed an innate good nature that not all his dandyism and the Carlisle tendency toward wildness could quite eradicate. He drank too much and was excessively expensive to maintain, but he seldom engaged in the scandals that were his elder brother's daily fare, and contented himself with being forever on the edge of financial ruin.

Lady Drewe was the youngest and the fairest of the three. She too possessed the pure Carlisle profile, but her hair was an enigma. None of her admirers could ever say quite what color it was, for it was neither pure gold, nor blond, nor tan, but an odd mixture of all three. It had the fascinating faculty of appearing sun-streaked even in the coldest of months, and had once inspired a poet to liken it to a sheaf of wheat at harvest. It was a conceit that met with much derision from the rest of her court, who thought it too commonplace a comparison for so beautiful a goddess. But if there was disagreement about the color of her unusual hair, no one, not even her more jealous rivals, could deny that her eyes were an astonishing and catlike amber.

Lady Drewe might not have gained the unsavory reputation of her elder brother Harry, but she was definitely fast. She was little more than twenty-one, but had long since dispensed with all female chaperonage, and indeed conducted herself as if all the protection of a marriage ring were hers. More than one concerned mama dreaded seeing her son fall into her beautiful coils, for she cared little for convention, had an abrupt way of speaking and an odd, almost mannish manner that men seemed to find entrancing, but shocked their mamas very much.

She was also outrageously expensive, did exactly as she pleased on every occasion, gambled to excess, and engaged in wild exploits very unsuited to a young woman of her birth. In short, she behaved very much as one would expect of a motherless girl raised in such a family. She also vented her temper as she chose, treated her admirers cavalierly, and one could only suppose culled her vocabulary from her brothers, for there could be no other explanation for some of the shocking expressions frequently to be heard on her lips.

Brothers and sister were not close, nor did their father, the indolent and hedonistic Earl of Wrexham, much trouble himself with his offspring. Owing to the differences in their ages, they had not grown up together, the boys being away at school most of the time. Whether for that reason or some other, there was little love lost among any of them.

Lady Drewe, motherless from infancy and left to the care of a series of ineffectual and indifferent nurses and governesses, had at one time annoyed her brothers very much by insisting upon tagging along after them on their holidays. But they had soon broken her of this ill-placed admiration by treating her in the same cavalier fashion they treated each other. Once, when she was ten, they had yielded to her demands to be included in their exploits and taken her for an illicit moonlight ride, only to abandon her without a qualm miles from home.

How she made it back again, neither of the brothers ever knew or troubled to find out. But she had appeared calmly at the breakfast table the next morning, and never revealed to anyone the unpleasant trick that had been played on her.

The brothers had for years played far worse tricks on each other. Harry, the elder, had once had his friends at Eton lock Charlie up in the coal cellar at the beginning of the Christmas holidays. It was only a coincidence that he was discovered before many hours, black from head to toe and fuming, and set free by an astonished porter. Otherwise Charlie would have been doomed to days of imprisonment there.

True to their own code, however, Charlie had not ratted on his brother either, but pretended he had somehow locked himself in. He had bided his time and gotten even the following term by delivering his brother up to a particularly vicious Latin master for not having his work done.

They also had a time-honored custom of outrageous wagers between them. Harry had once dared Charlie to jump a fence he had known to be crumbling on the far side. Charlie might easily have broken his neck, but instead merely broke his collarbone, though a valuable horse had had to be destroyed. In answer to Charlie's somewhat natural fury, Harry had merely shrugged and maintained that his brother had deserved it for being so rash as to blindly jump an unknown wall.

Charlie, more even-tempered than either his brother or sister, had in the end grown too fly to the time of day to be drawn in to either quarrels or wagers with his hot-headed siblings very often. But Drewe, as volatile as Harry, and every bit as competitive, could seldom resist. More conventional outsiders were sometimes shocked at the frank rivalry between them, but the simple truth was that none of them much liked the others and made little attempt to disguise the fact.

Lady Drewe said now in contempt, "Can't you be content with seducing other men's wives, without adding the young and innocent to your list?"

Lord Graydon yawned and produced his snuffbox. "It would seem not, my dear sister," he drawled. "At any rate, you will permit me to . . . ah . . . point out that it is really none of your business what I may choose to do."

If it occurred to any of them that this was a highly unsuitable topic for a young and unmarried sister, none of them betrayed it. Charlie, more attuned to social opinion than either of his siblings, and aware of the interested ears around them, did say irritably. "Dash it, at any rate this is hardly the place to discuss it."

"As near as I can tell, all of London has heard of it already," snapped Lady Drewe. "And it becomes my affair when you cause our name to be bandied about all over London."

"Really, my sweet, I had no idea you were so conventional."

She flushed at that, as he had meant her to, but Charlie resignedly shepherded them into a curtained alcove designed for dancers to rest in. "No sense airing our dirty linen in public," he said disapprovingly. "In fact, no sense airing it at all. We both know Harry will do exactly as he pleases. Which reminds me. Why the devil Bath?"

Harry looked momentarily surprised. "Why not? She had an ambition to go there."

"And you had an ambition to flaunt your conquest before the world!" said his sister contemptuously.

He shrugged. "Don't tell me you're shocked, my sweet?"

"No. Merely disgusted. I had at least given you credit for being above mere vulgarity."

That at least seemed to reach him. For a moment a muscle worked in his cheek and he looked briefly annoyed. "I must bow to your superior experience, my sweet. But in what way was I vulgar?"

"In every way. For the son of the Earl of Wrexham to engage in an affair of honor with the middle-aged and middle-class father of a *petite amie* that he meant to seduce and then abandon . . . ! Really, you must consider it a high point in your career."

For a moment longer he looked furious. Then he had recovered himself. "You will forgive me if this comes somewhat oddly from you, my pet," he retorted suavely. "I, at least, have not just jilted my second fiancé in as many months."

It was her turn to flush with fury. But Charlie said thoughtfully, "Oh, I don't know. Haymont was harmless enough, but Grenville ain't at all the sort of excrescence I'd like to have as a brother-in-law. Never thought Drewe should marry him, myself."

"I am loath to disagree with you, but I might point out that in that case she shouldn't have gotten engaged to him."

"Oh, well," said Charlie tolerantly. "Sort of thing that might happen to anyone."

"It might, but it doesn't. The truth is, you are annoyed because you know we are exactly alike, my sweet," Harry said with his pronounced sneer.

"You have finally managed to insult me!" she flashed back.

He merely laughed. "My poor pet. Have you met with some snubs tonight? Is that what's behind this uncharacteristic outrage? I hear Grenville is putting it about that he grew tired of you, not the other way round."

But that, at least, failed to meet its mark. "Do you really know me so little?" she demanded contemptuously.

"No, but I know your pride, m'dear. Really, now that I come to think of it, it is most selfish of me to create a new scandal just now. After all, my dear, your reputation is none too savory at the moment. It would be too bad if you were to find that not even your beauty emboldens a man to willingly take such a shrew to wife."

Her amber eyes sparked, but she said merely, "If I thought all men were like you, Harry, I would willingly die an old maid."

"You are bluffing. We both know you must marry to gain control of your fortune. It is, I will admit, a point of some resentment with me, since I am myself destined to rely on our father's nonexistent generosity. I have little doubt he will live to be a hundred, just to spite me. But it really would be a shame to let all that delicious money go to waste, especially considering how expensive you are. Is that a new gown, by the way? Vastly becoming."

"Stop trying to change the subject!"

"But it seems to me that *is* the subject. Really, you should have married Grenville after all. He may be an excrescence, as Charlie so delicately puts it, but he would have interfered with you as little as possible. And for you, you must admit, that would be a highly desirable trait in a husband."

Her face changed, revealing more than she intended, and she said too quickly, "Not even for that!"

Harry was watching her with sudden malicious interest. "Ah! I always wondered what was behind this latest break. It's not like you to repeat yourself, my sweet. What did he do? Flaunt his latest mistress in your face?"

"I don't wish to discuss it."

"Well, well," said Harry softly, pleased for some reason. "Don't tell me I have underestimated you all these years? It would be too distressing to discover you possess some scruples after all."

She had colored a little, but now she said almost wearily, "It's not likely, is it? I am a Carlisle, after all."

"You reassure me. But I begin to think it is time I interested myself in your affairs. Really, I fear I have been most remiss. You must know that they are betting in the clubs that after Grenville, few men will have the courage to offer for you. After all, two precipitately broken engagements is a little much, even for a Carlisle. In fact, I've noticed a sad diminution of your court tonight. Marchmont was nowhere to be seen, and Illingsworth has started to pay marked attention to that insipid little blond under Lady Holland's wing. Nor are they the only ones."

"Do you think I care for that?" she demanded.

"Not in the least. But perhaps you should. You are magnificent, my sweet, but not exactly every man's cup of tea. Take care you don't end up on the shelf, with all your beauty."

But that struck a nerve, for some reason. "Damn you!" she cried violently. "I will marry when and whom I please!"

His eyes shone with malicious mischief, pleased with the effect of his sally. "What odds do you lay me that you can't?" he inquired softly.

Charlie protested, but he might have spared his breath. Lady Drewe was too angry, and too naturally reckless, and the tradition of outrageous wagers was too well established between them for her to hesitate. "What you will!" she flashed back. "I will undertake to marry any man you name, in the time span you declare. Play or pay!"

2

"Devil take it! You're both mad!" Charlie protested.

"Oh, indubitably," Harry agreed, his eyes gleaming. "Fortunately I have just the candidate in mind."

Charlie forgot he had just pronounced the whole scheme mad. "Who is he?" he asked curiously.

"Oh, a protégé of Ponsonby's. He should be here tonight, so that you may see for yourself. I believe he's a Scots laird of some sort—calls himself the Earl of GlenRoss, though I have no doubt his estates consist of nothing but a few scraggy acres. All Scots are little better than barbarians."

"Too easy!" Lady Drewe said scornfully. "I don't bet on sure things."

"You are overconfident, my dear," Harry said in amusement. "Did you really think me turned philanthropist at this late date—or fool, for that matter? I have it on excellent authority that he profoundly disapproves of our rackety London ways. I believe all Scots are annoyingly straitlaced. This one's been in town for no more than a week, and already has gained the reputation of possessing little sense of humor and still less polish. Clift said he was insufferably rude to him, and he snubbed poor Caroline Wedmore for doing no more than flirting mildly with him. No, no, I promise you some amusing sport, my dear. He has scarcely scraped the mud off his unpolished boots, but still presumes to teach us our manners. He will disapprove of you on sight, my pet."

There was by now a distinct hint of curiosity in her unusual amber eyes. "How is it I haven't seen him before now?"

"I told you, he's devilish straitlaced. I fear he don't much appreciate our frivolous entertainments. More, he's in town only to raise a loan, so I understand. The Scots may despise us effete English, but they are always more than willing to take our gold." He eyed her with his unpleasant sneer. "Well, are you interested, my pet? I'll stake you my grays, which you have always coveted, against the emeralds you have on tonight that you can't get an offer from this clodpole before Christmas. Play or pay, as you say."

She was indeed looking speculative, but she said instantly, "I don't buy any horse sight unseen, Harry—especially from you! Did you think I had suddenly grown so green?"

He grinned. "Oh, I think you will take him, my pet. You never could resist a challenge."

Charlie, who had veered back to disapproval and had been listening to this with strong disgust, said irritably now, "Here, you ain't going to let Harry choose your husband for you, you madcap? Damme if I would!"

"If it comes to that, he could hardly do worse than I have so far," she countered impatiently.

"Aye, and that's put me in mind of something else," he objected. "Harry's at least right that your reputation won't stand another broken engagement, my girl."

"Then I'll marry the fool!" she said flippantly. "What you don't seem to understand is that I'm sick to death of my life of late! And Harry is also right that I'll never have any freedom until I gain control of my own fortune. Given that, what odds whom I marry? One husband seems about as good—or bad!—as any other. Now, we had best go back. We have been gone far too long already."

From that stance Charlie could not move her, but he was given very little opportunity, since as soon as they returned to the ballroom she was instantly surrounded by her usual court. A number seemed inclined to be indignant that she should have been monopolized for so long by a mere brother, and chaffed Charlie for being a dog in the manger.

Charlie, very used to this sort of thing, thought cynically that if Harry was right and there was a diminution in her court, it was hard to discover it. It seemed to him that half the fools in London were in love with his sister. Certainly she was always surrounded, as now, by a laughing throng of admirers, while other, less fortunate girls sat with their chaperones, trying not to look envious.

He was shrewd enough to know that envy had a good deal to do with her rather unsavory reputation. But, like Harry, she seemed unable—or unwilling—to resist going her outrageous length. All of the Carlisles were prone to scandal, but it was as if some devil drove her, as it did Harry. It was as if she had to prove something to the world, and Charlie had long since given up trying to understand her.

He had little doubt she would undertake this latest challenge—damn Harry for putting her up to it! Harry, Charlie knew, was motivated by nothing more than his annoying love of making mischief, but Drewe had never yet learned not to flare up at his taunts and insults. It was exactly the sort of hoydenish trick that, were it ever to become known, would set up the backs of all the biddies who already disapproved of her, and would go far toward ruining her. No strictly reared young woman would ever think of lending herself to such an ill-bred wager. In fact, if she didn't watch out, deuce take it, she would end by making London too hot to hold her, as Harry seemed set on doing.

Charlie, his thoughts vaguely uneasy, failed to remember to search again for the handsome brunette. It did not look to him as if Drewe's court had suffered any diminution, but then, he knew that flirting was one thing, serious intent quite another. It was true that a number of men who had once seemed devoted to Drewe had fallen away. Whether that was because they knew they stood no chance with the Golden Beauty, or whether Harry was right and she was indeed damaging her reputation by her caprice, it was hard for Charlie to know. Naturally, no one would say anything to him, and it was not much in the nature of any of the Carlisles to concern themselves for any other, so that he had paid very little attention to his sister's career.

He vowed vaguely to exert himself to change that, and then, characteristically shrugging off the annoying problem, wandered into the dice room.

Unfortunately, his luck proved to be quite out, and he soon wandered back to the ballroom, beginning to be aware of the amount of brandy he had drunk.

The company had by then retired to supper, and he soon found his sister, still surrounded by her usual throng. They were the life and soul of the party, and most eyes sooner or later drifted to that lively table, as often as not in vague disapproval. Two of her court were apparently vying with each other for the honor of cooling Lady Drewe's heated cheeks with her own fan, for Holyoke, one of the most determined of her suitors, soon succeeded in taking possession of the trifle of silk and painted sticks, and began determinedly to fan her with it, fending off the determined assault of young Lord Willoughby.

Charlie saw critically that his sister would seem to have attached a new and most distinguished member to her court. Lavisse, a rather recent émigré *comte,* had taken the *ton* by storm, both because of his polished Gallic air and his extreme good looks.

But it would seem he was indeed *épris,* for even as Charlie watched, Lavisse sprang up, and with mock ferocity loudly threatened to call out young Holyoke for the honor of

claiming one of the slightly crushed flowers from Lady
Drewe's corsage.

He was jesting, of course, and Charlie, very used to this
kind of display where his sister was concerned, was turning
away when his eye was caught by a pair of newcomers just
entering the supper room. They had paused in the doorway,
and like a good many others in the room, had been attracted
by the commotion surrounding Lady Drewe.

The first was a figure well known to Charlie, if only
casually, for it belonged to a member of the government
renowned for his sober good sense. Sir Richard Ponsonby
was serious, practical, and considered devoted to duty, and
as such had little to do with any Carlisle. He also was said
to have an unexpected sympathy for the common worker,
and had fought strenuously against the recent Combination
Act, which forbade the getting together or "combining" of
any two workers for the purpose of obtaining increased wages
or better working conditions.

Charlie's interest, however, was all for the second, a total
stranger. The newcomer had paused and bent his tall head
attentively to hear something his companion was saying, but
his very blue eyes rested coolly on Drewe. He himself was
considerably above average height, and it may have been
that that made him stand out in the room. But he looked subtly
out of place. He had a somewhat dark complexion with a
pair of piercing blue eyes set below fine dark brows, in an
age when the whiteness of a man's skin was hardly less
valued than that of a lady. And it also occurred to Charlie,
for some reason, that he would have looked more at home
on the deck of a ship, or with a sword in his hand, than in
a crowded ballroom.

Then Charlie shook himself, wondering what had
possessed him to become so fanciful. It could only be the
brandy, for on second glance the newcomer devolved into

nothing more than a slightly unfashionable stranger. His evening clothes were well-cut but by no means in the latest exaggerated style, and though his dark hair was fashionably cropped, it gave no hint of the careful arrangement it had taken Charlie himself almost an hour to achieve.

Graydon's voice sounded unexpectedly and maliciously in his ear. "Admiring the candidate, little brother? You must admit he's far more passable than you expected. Quite good-looking, in fact, if you like the brutish type."

"Good God, you might as well make Drewe a present of your grays!" said Charlie frankly. "He won't stand a chance against her."

"Perhaps. But I think you're wrong. Watch."

As they stood there, Sir Richard Ponsonby caught sight of someone he knew among Drewe's court. He hesitated, then took his companion over, performing general introductions. The newcomer made a polite bow to Drewe, but there was no appreciable admiration or interest in his vivid blue eyes, and he turned almost immediately away to address a remark to someone else.

Harry smiled, well pleased with himself, for whether they approved or disapproved of her, few men were unmoved by Drewe's beauty.

"Lord, that don't mean anything!" Charlie insisted scathingly. "He was watching her from across the room earlier. And even I have to admit she's plaguily irresistible when she chooses to be!"

"Just wait," Harry said again, his sneer very much in place.

Drewe, in the meantime, unaware of her interested audience, had not immediately caught the murmured name. She said in her abrupt way, "I'm sorry. Are you Lord GlenRoss?"

The newcomer had turned away, but he turned politely back at that, and bowed slightly. "I have that dubious honor. But I can't flatter myself your ladyship has heard of me." He spoke with a slight burr that was not displeasing.

She subjected him to one of her frank stares. "I fancy I heard your name mentioned somewhere. Are you enjoying the ball? An insipid squeeze, isn't it?"

"I think so. But from the looks of it, I would have said that you were enjoying yourself very well, my lady."

His meaning was clear and hardly flattering, and her beautiful eyes narrowed swiftly. She was not used to receiving snubs, certainly not from country bumpkins, and her curiosity was definitely piqued.

In fact, she would almost have believed she had misunderstood him had she not encountered a far-from-admiring gleam in his very blue eyes as he looked down at her.

Suddenly very much on her mettle, she drawled, "You would seem to hold our provincial amusements cheap, my lord. No doubt they are more to your taste in your own country?"

Lord Holyoke had turned to listen, for he knew that expression in his idol's face. He glanced swiftly to the Scotsman but the Scotsman seemed not to realize he was in danger. "You misunderstand me, my lady," he said, sounding merely amused. "I fear I am not one for social gatherings like this in either country."

Holyoke glanced swiftly back to Lady Drewe, wondering who was this barbaric Scotsman? He had abominable manners, whoever he was. Did he know whom he was talking to?

But Drewe was regarding him with a frowning interest she did not show many men. Holyoke thought she had never looked more beautiful, and forgot the Scotsman in his admiration of his goddess.

"Then I wonder you should not have excused yourself, my lord," she retorted silkily. "In England at least, we hold it bad manners to criticize one's hostess."

He bowed again, but made no reply. The next moment Sir Richard said something to him, and they had withdrawn.

Drewe stared after him, her eyes narrowed and dangerous. But she was never so reckless as when she knew herself to be disapproved, and so became even more the life and soul of the party. When Lavisse whispered something mockingly in her ear, she did not hesitate to strip off one of her gloves and offer her slender wrist to him.

He laughed and demonstrated how a gentleman took snuff from a lady's wrist on the Continent. Her court protested laughingly, but there were several shocked gasps from nearby onlookers. Drewe ignored those, but she had the intense satisfaction of knowing she had one other observer to this outrageous act; when she lifted her eyes just as Lavisse bent provocatively over her wrist, she found the Scotsman's gaze on her.

Their eyes met for an instant, her's full of challenge. He hesitated, then lifted his glass toward her, whether in silent toast or amusement, she could not tell. Then he had turned away again, and disappeared in the crowded room.

To her own surprise, Drewe felt the hot blood invade her cheeks and scarcely heard the clamor around her for others to try the trick. She might care nothing for the world's opinion, but she had read, unmistakably, distinct contempt in the Scotsman's eyes before he had turned away. For the rest of the evening, there remained a tight, bright look in her eyes, and she pleaded a headache and left at an unusually early hour. On the drive home, she demanded abruptly, "Is the wager still open, Harry?"

Harry laughed. "I thought you would be intrigued, my pet. Snubbed you, did he?"

"He did, but he shall be made to learn his mistake," she said dangerously. "Until Christmas, I think you said?"

"Oh, excellent! But you would be advised to look to your laurels, my sweet. I warn you, this is one man you won't subjugate with your temper and caprice."

"You would do better to look to your own grays," she retorted. "I have always driven them better than you do anyway."

Harry laughed again. "Then may the best man win," he said maliciously.

Drewe shrugged her beautiful shoulders in the dark. "If that is meant to be insulting, it misses the mark," she said contemptuously. "I am a better man than you are, Harry."

3

Lady Drewe might at least have been reassured to know she had succeeded in making more of an impression on the newcomer than he had wished her to believe. As they strolled home a few minutes later, GlenRoss inquired idly about the beauty all in amber who was so obviously the center of attention at the ball.

Sir Richard, who disapproved on principle of frivolous beauties, pricked up his ears and said warningly, "Egad, I knew it was a mistake to present you. If you'll take my advice, my boy, you won't get caught in her net."

The other laughed. "I'm not likely to, sir. Even were I tempted—which I'm not—I doubt I would appeal to the lady."

Sir Richard glanced at him in the darkness, and privately thought his young guest underrated his own appeal. He had seen more than one female at the ball that night glance in the Scot's direction with undeniable interest, and there could be no doubt that Lady Drewe Carlisle had shown him unexpected encouragement.

Not that that was a matter for congratulation, of course, for Sir Richard had no wish to see the boy caught in her toils. "Even so, I'd advise you not to tempt fate, Ian," he said frankly. "Wiser heads than yours have fallen victim to her fatal charm, God knows."

"That I don't doubt," said GlenRoss in amusement. "But

fortunately I have neither the time nor the inclination to dance attendance on a spoilt English beauty. I will confess only to curiosity. Who is she?''

''Oh, Wrexham's youngest,'' offered Ponsonby grudgingly. ''Wild as bedamned, of course. You saw her. All of the Carlisles are, come to that. I hear Graydon's just committed some new scandal involving a middle-class gel. Nearly killed the father, so I'm told. 'Fore Gad, there's bad blood there. Wrexham's just as bad. Makes no bones about his decadent life, and concerns himself as little as possible with his offspring. Pays their debts when he has to, and little else. But to their credit—or perhaps their ruination—they are all remarkably handsome, I'll at least give them that. In truth, I'd hate to see any man caught in her toils, but she'd ruin you, my boy.''

They walked on for several moments in silence. It was a chilly evening, and most people out at that late hour had taken a hansom or a chair, so that they had the way mostly to themselves. After a moment Ponsonby added, as if his mind was still on the subject despite his professed disapproval, ''Though I'll grant you she's unexpectedly taking, even to an old and staid fool like me. Undeniably beautiful, of course, but it doesn't seem to have gone to her head, as it does with most accredited beauties. I can almost find it in me to feel sorry for her, if she weren't so dangerous. From all I can tell, her upbringing was damnable, for her mother died when she was a baby, and Wrexham seems to have relied upon a series of nannies and governesses to raise her. Worse, her two brothers are some of our worst young Mohocks, and seem more to egg her on than protect her.''

He shook his head. ''In fact, she seems to have been raised more boy than a girl, which, come to think of it, is not all bad. All I know is that she possesses surprisingly few feminine wiles, for all her beauty. You saw her tonight. She's

forever surrounded by admirers, but is impatient of compliments, so I hear, and seems to treat most of her admirers
cavalierly. She certainly can outride, outdrive, and even out-
shoot most of her court.''

He chuckled. ''Outcurse them too, so I understand, when
she's in a temper. Been engaged twice and broke off both
engagements shortly before the weddings, with no other
explanation than that she'd changed her mind. If you ask me,
it's a strong man—or a fool—who will take her in hand.''

His companion shrugged. ''Console yourself, sir. It
certainly won't be me. I never had the smallest desire to
compete for a lady's favors, especially where they're given
so freely. And I've enough on my plate as it is. The last thing
I need is to take some imperious English beauty home with
me.''

Ponsonby relaxed, reassured. He had been half-afraid he
had said too much and would merely pique his young
companion's interest, but it seemed the Scot had a solid head
on his shoulders, as Ponsonby had already discovered. ''Aye,
she'd lead you a merry dance,'' he agreed with a chuckle.
''I pity the poor man who finally weds her. What did you
think of Gilchrist, the man I took you to meet, by the by?
He could prove useful to you.''

After that the conversation drifted naturally to other
matters, and neither spoke of the spoiled beauty again.
Ponsonby went to bed some time later with the comforting
feeling that he had successfully negotiated an unexpected
shoal. He liked young GlenRoss and would hate to see him
brought to ruin by a beautiful baggage. But it was doubtful
if their paths would cross again, especially if he had anything
to do with it.

Unfortunately for Ponsonby's peace of mind, Lady Drewe

and his protégé met the very next morning, by complete accident, in the park.

Lady Drewe had the habit of riding at an early hour, no matter how late she might have been out the night before, since she despised the crowds at the more fashionable hour of promenade and had no patience for a gentle canter in the park. Her usual style was neck-or-nothing, and she rode a magnificent black that no one would have considered a suitable lady's mount. She had also long since dispensed with an escort, since she usually had the park to herself at that hour and found a groom an annoying constraint.

She was returning from an invigorating gallop when she saw another solitary horseman on a rattail gray coming leisurely toward her. Her first reaction was one of annoyance, for she guarded her private rides jealously, and had no desire to have them ruined by any of her court.

When she recognized who the newcomer was, however, a thoughtful look came into her eyes and she deliberately spurred toward him.

For his part, GlenRoss seemed to hesitate, which was far from flattering, then pulled up easily as he reached her. He was dressed that morning in buckskins and a well-cut blue coat that became him better than evening dress had done the night before. "You're out early, my lady," he remarked pleasantly. "That is somehow not in keeping with my notion of a fashionable London beauty."

He spoke with a faint burr, but with none of the exaggerated accent she might have expected. Nevertheless she lifted her chin faintly, reading condemnation in his words. "Then you know nothing of us," she said bluntly.

"That at least is true," he agreed in amusement. He looked her black over with more interest than he had yet shown her and added, "I saw you earlier, as a matter of fact. You are clearly a notable horsewoman, but your style is . . . er . . .

somewhat precipitate for a city park, wouldn't you say?''

"And yours is for whipsters!'' she retorted inexcusably. "I have little use for park jauntering. It seems Scotland is not as wild as I was led to believe.''

She had meant to be insulting, but he merely threw back his head and laughed, the sound untrammeled on the chill morning air. "Oh, we've more sense than to waste either our energy or our mount's on mere exercise,'' he said with a twinkle. "There are unfortunately too many times when we've no choice in the matter.''

It was certainly not the answer she expected, and she frowned a little, taken off-guard. "Why not?'' she demanded after a moment.

"Ah. I fear pony reiving has always been a favorite pastime in the Highlands, and we're no' so civilized that it's unknown even now. We're also a lazy people, I believe. We've little inclination to find extra work for ourselves, and no need for additional exercise.''

It was said quite cheerfully, and Drewe was a little taken aback. Harry had condescendingly called all Scotsmen barbarians, and she certainly had not expected this one to more or less admit it. "Then what are you doing now?'' she demanded suspiciously.

"Waiting for someone. And as a people we've precious little patience for that either, I fear. I was just about to give up when I saw you.''

She was nothing if not audacious, and so challenged in her abrupt way, "Or because you saw me, perhaps? Why the devil did you dare to snub me last night?''

To give him credit, he did not hang back from so direct an attack. "Did I? I was not aware of it. Or that you would have noticed if I had. But I was told your language descended to the stables whenever you were annoyed.''

"By Ponsonby, I suppose?" She sneered. "Do you think I care what is said of me?"

"That, also, I was told," he said in amusement.

This was too much! Her eyes flashed becomingly and she said, goaded, "Upon my word, you are insolent! Nor was I mistaken last night. You do have the effrontery to disapprove of me, confound you!"

He hesitated, then shrugged. "You are mistaken. I have neither the right nor enough interest to disapprove of you, my lady. But it was clear to me, from our admittedly brief acquaintance, that you deliberately invite disapproval. I wonder you should be surprised when you achieve your goal."

As she gaped, white-lipped with fury, he nodded and turned his gray and left her.

A lesser gamester than Lady Drewe might have given up at that point, but opposition always merely made her the more determined. He—an uncivilized Scot!—had twice dared to snub her, and that was a thing not to be allowed. If she had ever entertained any scruples about deliberately subjugating him for her own amusement, she was now easily able to repress them. GlenRoss clearly deserved to be brought down a peg or two, and she was just the one to do it.

Certainly, when issued so direct a challenge, it was not within her to cry craven. She determined to bring him to heel, and began accordingly to weave her plans. He should be made to fall willingly at her feet, and then and only then would she be satisfied.

Despite her beauty, she did not believe herself inordinately vain, and in truth despised the majority of her slavish court. But no man, and especially not an ignorant Scot, should be allowed to so clearly find Lady Drewe Carlisle wanting. The same spirit that as a child had led her to throw her heart into any challenge laid down by her brothers, however outrageous—and frequently at the risk of her neck or limbs—now refused to allow her to back down.

Unfortunately, GlenRoss seemed to have as little taste for social events as he claimed, for it was almost a full week before she saw her quarry again. Surprisingly enough, that was at an evening gaming party, hosted by one of the most notorious gamesters in London, Lady Lowecroft, and thus not a place Drewe had even considered finding so straitlaced a newcomer.

Still, the meeting was perhaps unfortunate, for many people, not only straitlaced Scots, disapproved of the current rage for gaming among women. Indeed, Drewe was briefly annoyed, for though she had been longing for the meeting, he seemed always to catch her in an unflattering moment.

Drewe, herself an inveterate gambler, was enjoying a run of extraordinary luck at faro, to the complaint of her usual throng, who swore she was fleecing them unmercifully. She was not bored for once, and thus looking her best, the usual discontent absent from her beautiful face.

She was laughing and claiming her winnings when she chanced to look up and met GlenRoss's cool blue eyes on her from across the room.

But since it played no part of her plans to alter herself in any way to suit his gothic notions of propriety, and she meant to bring him to her feet even though he disapproved of her, she lifted her chin and stared challengingly at him.

He disarmed the challenge by bowing slightly and turning away, leaving her more annoyed than ever.

It would seem to have affected her game, or else her mind was not on her play, for her luck turned then. She had soon lost back all her winnings, and even the gold bangle on her wrist, studded with diamonds. It was Lavisse who won it, but he gallantly offered to stake everything against one kiss.

It was the sort of wager that in the past might have appealed to her, but she discovered that for some reason tonight she had lost her enjoyment. "Another time, perhaps! I am grown bored," she said in her abrupt way. "Pray continue without me."

Lavisse looked to be a little taken aback, but the rest of her court was used to her cavalier treatment. They automatically set up a storm of protest, but she ignored them all and went off to find some champagne.

There she encountered GlenRoss standing in the doorway to the refreshment room. "My lord!" she said briefly, clearly meaning to pass through.

He bowed civilly. "My lady. It would seem you have left your friends desolate."

She shrugged. "I fear my luck was quite out."

"I am sorry to hear it. You seemed to be enjoying a remarkable run of luck earlier."

She regarded him with her clear, critical gaze. "You do not play? Or is gaming yet another thing you disapprove of, my lord?"

"I have better things to do with my money, yes," he agreed, in no whit thrown out of countenance.

"I wonder, then, you should have attended a gaming party!" she rejoined tartly. "Or did you merely come to stand around and be disagreeable?"

He bowed again, his lips twitching. "It would seem losing does not agree with you, my lady. That being the case, I will take myself off and leave you to recover your spirits."

She could have stamped her foot in rage.

She met him again two days later, at a rout-party, where he nodded from across the room but did not approach her; and then again at a ball at Lady Richmond's on Friday. This time he was but a few yards from her, and could not ignore a summons from her eyes. He approached and bowed politely. "Lady Drewe."

"Lord GlenRoss. You do not dance either, I see. Now, why am I not surprised to learn that?"

His lips twitched again, but he answered gravely enough, "I do, when pressed. But I confess I've little enough patience with it."

"I have no doubt you've far more important matters to concern you," she said acidly.

He bowed again. "No. Say rather that I've little enough skill at it, and so have no wish to betray myself."

She was a little taken off-guard, despite herself. "I feel sure you are too modest. You do not ride in the mornings any longer?"

"No. I assumed that had you wished for an escort you would have had one. It cannot be easy in this madhouse to find a moment's privacy, and being one who values my own, I would not for the world intrude on anyone else's. But I must not keep you. Your court will be wondering where you have gotten to."

Her brows rose and she said challengingly, "You mean that you wish to go! Pray don't wrap it up in clean linen for my account, sir!"

He smiled maliciously. "Being so outspoken yourself, my lady, I made sure you would not mind a little plain speaking in others. The truth is, I'm not yet used to London hours, and I've a business appointment early in the morning. You will excuse me, I hope?"

She stared wrathfully after him, torn between annoyance and a grudging respect. She might almost believe she had met her match at last.

4

In fact, it occurred to Drewe that GlenRoss somehow knew of the wager and was deliberately trying to thwart her.

She might almost have suspected Harry was playing a double game and taxed him with the matter, except that however loose his morals might be otherwise, in all aspects of play Harry was surprisingly scrupulous. And GlenRoss could not know of so unlikely a wager otherwise. No, he was merely being insufferably pompous, but they would see who had the last laugh!

It was an added annoyance, of course, that Harry knew of her plans and was following her lack of progress with malicious satisfaction. He twitted her about it over the breakfast table the next morning, saying, "I really fear the barbarian holds all the honors so far, my pet. I can't remember when I was last so amused. Or do you care to admit defeat now, and be done with it?"

"I have until Christmas," she reminded him irritably.

"Yes, but that is fast approaching, my sweet. In fact, if I were not in such embarrassing financial difficulties, I would not for the world end so amusing a farce. It is quite a new come-out for you to find someone wholly immune to your famous charms. Confess it, you have made no headway with him at all."

"Don't count me out until Christmas," she snapped, and strode out without finishing her breakfast.

* * *

But for once luck favored her, for as she was driving toward the park the next day, she saw GlenRoss walking toward her, quite alone.

She was accustomed to drive herself in her own perch phaeton behind a pair of glossy and mettlesome chestnuts, by no means a conventional equipage for a lady. Her admirers clamored to be taken up beside her, but she granted the honor to very few, saying frankly that she had no wish to be distracted by annoying chatter just as she was feathering a corner or needed her concentration to pass another vehicle.

But this time she hesitated only an instant before pulling up and saying briskly, "Good morning! Do you care to take a turn around the park with me, my lord?"

As he hesitated, she added mockingly, "You needn't fear I will overturn you! Or is riding with females yet another thing you don't do?"

In the face of so direct a challenge she was not surprised when he shrugged and climbed up to join her in the awkward vehicle. "I have not the least fear you will overturn me," he said frankly as he watched her give her team the office and weave expertly through the heavy traffic on Piccadilly. "Lady Drewe Carlisle's skill with the ribbons, as with so many other things, is justly famous. In fact, this is indeed an honor, for I didn't think you condescended to take up passengers in the usual way."

"I don't! In fact, I must ask you not to speak to me until we are out of this traffic, or I will overturn you."

He looked amused, but since her pair was obviously very fresh, was obligingly silent until she had turned in between the gates into the park. Then he said merely, "It would seem your skill was not exaggerated. But would not a gentler pair serve you better in the city? But that question no doubt shows my ignorance. It would certainly draw less attention to you."

She flushed and said shortly, "I can handle this or any other pair."

She deliberately allowed the chestnuts to lengthen their stride, hoping he would betray some uneasiness, for she was well aware that most men disliked being driven by a woman. They seldom could quite prevent themselves from tensing and keeping a wary eye on the road.

But to her annoyance, GlenRoss did not make that error. Either he possessed nerves of steel or he did indeed trust her skill, for he seemed perfectly at his ease.

"Is driving something else Scots don't do, unless necessary?" she demanded provocatively, keeping her eyes on the road ahead.

He laughed. "Oh, we've an appreciation of the skill. But I must confess that where I live, the roads are shockingly bad, so there's little call for it."

She turned to look at him in surprise. "Good God! Where do you live?"

"I doubt you've heard of it. It's in the north, above Edinburgh. You would no doubt find it the back of beyond."

"And is it?"

"Oh, aye, but that has had its advantages more often than not. Especially when the English have come in search of us for one reason or another," he said in amusement.

She turned again to look at him, assessing him as if for the first time. "You are a strange man," she said abruptly. "And you talk as if the English and Scots weren't one people. Aren't we all British now?"

"On paper," he admitted. "But I confess it's not that easy where I come from, and you must admit the prejudice is not all on our side. In fact, since coming to London I've begun to wonder if I haven't sprouted two heads and a forked tail myself."

It was near enough to the truth to again throw her off her guard. It was not a common experience for her. She gathered her wits and countered, "Don't tell me you're not just as bad. You came here expecting to disapprove of all you saw. Didn't you?"

"Perhaps, but then, that's a different matter entirely," he said gravely. "It's well known that all Sassanach are a weak and rapacious lot, with naught on their minds but keeping their heels on the heads of more godly Scots. We've a right to our prejudices."

It took her a moment to realize he was teasing her. Against her will, she realized she liked the way his well-chiseled mouth pulled up when he was amused, and the engaging twinkle in his vivid blue eyes.

"Are all Scots like you?" she demanded frankly.

"Heaven forbid. I'm something of a disgrace, I fear. I'm not above trafficking with our ancient enemy, you see, and that is far from being universally appreciated where I come from."

"Oh, come now! England and Scotland have been united now for almost a hundred years."

"Aye. But for all that I jest, Culloden might not have been fifty years ago in many Scots' minds. We've never learned to like defeat, I fear."

She saw that he had sobered, and wondered if that might be behind his remarkable resistance to her. It was something to consider, but now she protested, "But that was long before we were born."

"Yes, but we Scots have long memories. We've had a great many wrongs to resent over the centuries, you see. We've learned the way of it by now."

This was very different from the conversation she had expected, but she discovered she was interested, and so asked curiously, "Do you feel that way too?"

He shrugged. "I prefer to live in the present. At any rate, beggars can't be choosers. I've need of English support."

She was again startled that he would speak so openly of something she would have regarded as shameful. "You came to borrow money, I understand," she announced coolly.

"Aye, there's that too, if I can," he admitted readily. "But I've come for favors before gold."

That caught her attention again. "Favors? What kind of favors?"

But it seemed his confidences were at an end. "It seems to me that my critics would be justified in calling me a gaumless Scot," he said in amusement. "You've less than no interest in my affairs, and this is indeed a foolish conversation to be having with a pretty lass."

It was the first time he had paid her a compliment of any sort, and she should have felt triumphant. Instead she was impatient. "Oh, the devil! Don't spoil it!" she said impulsively.

He looked a little startled. "Spoil it? Spoil what?"

"You were conversing with me as if I actually possessed a brain! But I should have known it was too good to last," she said contemptuously.

He eyed her with new interest. "And that is somehow not a thing I would expect the beautiful Lady Drewe Carlisle to say."

"But then, you know very little about me."

He smiled in a more genuine way than she had yet seen him. "That at least is quite true," he confessed. "Less even than I thought, obviously. And it's said we Scots have the devil's own tact. But in this case I meant only, in my clumsy way, that my business in London is both complicated and uncommonly tedious, and I'd no wish to bore you with it."

"You mean for once you had no intention of insulting me!" she said bluntly. "And I'll tell you when I'm bored."

He almost choked. "Something tells me that you will, my lady," he agreed gravely, then shrugged. "And it's just as well. Like most Scots, I fear I've a fondness for the sound of my own voice, and like nothing better than talking of my own affairs. You're rash to encourage me. In fact, it's a fairly long and tedious story, but in brief, I wish to import the weaving industry into my glens, and you English have both the gold and the knowledge we need."

It was hardly the answer she had expected. "Weaving? Good God, whatever for?"

"Ah, that gets into the complicated part. Suffice it to say that too many of the Highland people these days are dirt poor. I know it is the common belief here that that has always been the case, but appearances can be deceptive. Now, however, they're being forced out of the glens, either to Edinburgh or Glasgow to starve, or across the seas to America in indentured servitude. I've a vain dislike of seeing my Frasers among them."

"Your Frasers? Who are they?" she demanded, frowning a little.

"It's a manner of speaking, only. But generally, though the English have done their best to destroy the clan system, most of my tenants and dependents are related to me in some way. I'm their hereditary chieftain, and they have the legal right to look to me to redress their ills. It doubtless sounds hopelessly feudal to you, but it has been the way in Scotland for over a thousand years. Unfortunately, no English edicts or concerted attempts to break up the clans have persuaded those who have lived with the system all their lives to rely on Southern law instead. Especially since little provision is made in it for them."

She was far from understanding, and felt uncharacteristically ignorant. After a moment he said lightly, "I warned you it was a complicated subject, and one I'm not to be trusted on. And it seems we have reached the gate again.''

She had been so engrossed in what he had been saying that she had not noticed. She would have liked to ask him a great many more questions, but she had achieved more than she had dared hope, and so would not hold him. ''And that is why you have come to London, and look down on us English so much?'' she inquired curiously, obediently pulling up.

''Since I have come with my hat in hand, I hope I am not so foolish as to look down upon you,'' he said lightly, preparing to climb down. ''Thank you for a most enjoyable drive, Lady Drewe.''

She was strangely loath to see him go, for some reason. ''May I not drop you somewhere? I am going back in that direction.''

He grinned up at her, having reached the ground. ''No, no, I have presumed on the great honor you have done me too much already by prosing on about my own affairs. At any rate, I see my man there waiting for me.''

She saw that a short, stout figure was indeed waiting patiently at the gate, looking somewhat fiercely out at her from very blue eyes in a weather-beaten face. ''Is he your groom?'' she asked curiously.

''Duncan?'' He seemed amused by the idea. ''No, he's my kinsman, servant, companion, conscience—you name it. Pay no attention to his scowl. He looks that way all the time.''

She leaned over and held out her hand in her forthright way. ''I begin to believe you are as dangerous as your ancestors were reputed to be, my lord,'' she said truthfully. ''You have certainly succeeded in throwing me off balance, which I assure you is no easy thing to do. Do you go to Lady Dawlish's ball? Perhaps I will see you there.''

"I don't think so," he said with an odd gentleness.

She flushed, for he had behaved so naturally that he had indeed thrown her off her guard, so that the snub was all the worse. "I see! You should not try your luck too far, my lord!" she warned, annoyed once more.

He laughed and took her hand. "No, no. I only meant that I have business affairs that evening. What's more, I regret that I am unacquainted with the lady.''

She shook her head and said bluntly, "You are not very complimentary. Any other man would have moved heaven and earth to obtain an introduction after such an opening.''

"Nay, lass, I'm no cavalier. Did you think it?" he asked in amusement. "You must content yourself with having the rest of London at your feet." He stepped back from the phaeton, leaving her again torn between anger and reluctant admiration of his superior methods.

But Lord GlenRoss was indeed aware of the lady's purpose, and was playing a deep and amusing game of his own. As he approached his kinsman, the dour Duncan remarked in broadest Scots, "Take care ye're no' forgettin' yer business here, wi' the likes o' that.''

GlenRoss laughed. "I'm not likely to. And you're far from approving of my business anyway.''

"I hold little with traffic with the heathen English," Duncan muttered dourly. "And still less with gowden Jezebels such as her. Who is she?''

"The Lady Drewe Carlisle. Quite above my touch, I assure you. You needn't worry.''

Duncan looked skeptical. "It didna look it. I've no trust in any English, come to that."

"Well, you may trust this one," GlenRoss said in amusement. "I will admit it piques her that I haven't fallen at her feet, but believe me, she would sooner fly than throw herself away on an ignorant Scot. You should know it is all a game with them. I believe she has set out to teach me a lesson, and that amuses me, but we are neither of us in any danger of forgetting ourselves."

Duncan grunted and fell into step beside him. After a moment GlenRoss added with a wicked grin, "Unfortunately, I annoy the lady so much she is hard pressed to remember that she meant to enthrall me, and usually ends by picking a quarrel with me whenever we meet. And you know me. I ever had a deplorable habit of pricking pretension where I find it. I regret to say I am enjoying myself hugely."

"Take care it's no' ye who are pricked," Duncan warned sourly. "I'll feel safer when we're home again, a' the same."

"Why, so will I. I will confess London suits me but little." Then GlenRoss grinned again. "I will also confess if I must that Lady Drewe Carlisle is not unappealing when she forgets to be the grand lady. But I've no more use for a spoilt English bride than she has for a penniless Scots husband. Surely you've not been in England all this time without discovering they still think we all eat with knives and murder each other for sport?"

"I've seen enough of both in my time, come to that," Duncan muttered. "But I'll still be safer awa' from this gaumless place."

"That's because you are an ignorant Scot and clearly know no better," retorted his master. "Lady Drewe Carlisle would find our home an uncivilized wasteland and would flee screaming back to London within a fortnight. It is inconceivable to her we could be anxious to leave civilized London to return there.''

screaming back to London within a fortnight all escort
ceivable to her... would bore... to death... and London
to rest... long past.

5

Drewe went to Lady Dawlish's ball, but she was surprised
to discover how little lure it suddenly held for her. The notion
that it was because GlenRoss was not to be there irritated
her so much that she wore a new and exceedingly expensive
gown for the occasion. But for once it could not be said that
Lady Drewe Carlisle was the life and soul of the party.

She was, in fact, experiencing something of a revelation.
She had entered into the ridiculous wager out of pique, and
pursued it simply to teach GlenRoss a lesson. But she had
not expected to find herself being inexplicably drawn to the
barbarous Scot.

Unfortunately, she had discovered that when he cared to
put himself to the trouble, he could be oddly likable. He had
a wry, self-deprecating humor, seemingly more than his share
of wit, and an unexpected capacity to amuse her even as he
was most annoying her. More, it would seem he had purpose
and a goal to his life, which in her world was so rare as to
be almost unprecedented.

As for his dislike of London, she came closer to agreeing
with him than he might think. It was a long time since she
had looked forward to a social event with more than casual
boredom, and even longer since the idea of a flirtation had
been more than the tedious way one got through an evening.
It was expected of one, but by no means to be taken seriously.

Of late she had become so jaded she would willingly have

forgone most of the endless round of tedious social events she was expected to attend. But that would be to give ammunition to her critics, who since her last broken engagement had been looking for some sign of shame or self-consciousness on her part. And so she went out, night after night, to flirt outrageously and generally prove right the critics who claimed she had no heart.

Disapproval was nothing new, of course. She had lived with it all her life. GlenRoss had been right, damn him, to say that she even frequently cultivated it. Life was too tedious else, and God knew there was little enough to keep her amused otherwise. To shock the hidebound critics who disapproved so openly of her and her family had become almost a mission.

And what other choice had she ever had, if the truth be known? Her brothers were already notorious when she first arrived in London, and she was clearly expected to follow in their footsteps. Either that or spend her life trying to prove to a suspicious world that she was wholly unlike them, which would have been as tiring as it was demeaning, and involved disowning one's own heritage.

And to tell the truth, that reputation had been an advantage, all in all, for she'd little taste for playing the bread-and-butter miss. She'd dispensed with a chaperone, largely done as she wished, and led the *ton* for almost five years now, ever since she was seventeen. Few could boast as much.

But there was the rub, of course. It was perhaps an exaggeration to say she was at her last prayers, but it was true that she had begun to notice the passage of years. At first she had no intention of tying herself down, even though an early marriage would have put her in possession of her own fortune. She was enjoying her sudden freedom too much after her restricted and lonely childhood to think of giving any one person such power over her again.

But it was true—damn Harry to perdition for seeing it!— that over the years there had been a diminution in her court of the more reliable, steadfast man. At first she hadn't noticed, or told herself she didn't care, for men of virtue tended to bore her. But soon it became apparent even to her that her reputation had become such that the more respectable women hated to see their sons caught in her coils, and the more sober and sedate gentlemen thought her too dangerous to take for wife.

Gradually, though the number remained steady and she always found herself the center of attention, her admirers dwindled to a few predictable types: youthful boys who thought it the thing to be in love with her; married men who enlivened their boring lives by making fools of themselves over her; professional bachelors like her brothers who had no intention of marrying, or if they did, of being faithful to their wives; and the totally ineligible, who would have been delighted to wed her for her fortune and live on her coattails, but were wholly feckless themselves.

None of them would have made even passable husbands. Oh, there was, of course, the occasional more staid gentleman who fell in love with her almost against his will and despite all his relations' direst warnings. But even they were becoming increasingly few and far between, for her reputation for being both fast and completely heartless was far too well established.

At first she had not minded, and even reveled in her reputation. But it had not previously occurred to her that she was effectively painting herself into a corner that it would one day be almost impossible to extricate herself from.

When that realization first occurred to her she had panicked. She had declined so many offers over the years that she had lost count of them; but once knocked off her complacent pedestal, it had occurred to her that even some of her most determined suitors had dropped off. Her court had largely dwindled down to those she had refused time after time until it had become routine for both of them, and those hardened rakes who would have been shocked indeed if she had ever accepted them.

Shaken and realizing for the first time that time might be running out for her, she had had to face her own future squarely. Marriage had always loomed as some distant, faintly undesirable end, but she had always been unable to imagine herself married to anyone she knew. Either they adored her so thoroughly they would never have stood up to her, which she tended to despise; or they were men like her brothers, who, once married, would expect as little fidelity from her as they planned to give, and saw marriage merely as a matter of convenience.

Neither appealed to her, but of the two, she had preferred at least the semblance of sincerity. So she had become engaged to Haymont, a charming and good-natured young man of good family who had been touchingly awed by his good fortune.

That had been the trouble, of course. He had gone about in a daze of love, deferred to her in everything, and made her feel at first uncomfortable by his devotion, and then positively guilty. Unfortunately she was not of that pious nature that profited from feelings of guilt. It seldom endured long in her without turning into disgust, and she had in the end found herself despising her betrothed for his blind adoration.

There had been nothing to do but break it off, which had left her worse off than before. There had been a great deal of talk at the unexpected engagement, and a great deal more at its summary ending, and sympathy, not unnaturally, had not been on her side. In short, it had been a fiasco.

Shaken, but still facing the same dilemma, she had vowed

to go to the opposite extreme: someone who had no heart to be broken, and who would go into the marriage with as few delusions as she had.

That had been even easier to find, and so she had become engaged to Grenville. It was a time she shuddered even now to think of. She had quickly learned he was as debauched as he was vicious, and she had fled from that second engagement with no thought spared to the effect on her reputation this time. It had been bad, of course, but she had withstood all the gossip with a stoic face and counted herself lucky to have learned the truth in time.

That was why the thought of the distaste in GlenRoss's eyes that first night had been so infuriating. It had been temper, and an unworthy desire to stop Harry's foul taunts, that had led her to agree to the wager, for if he had noticed, she could be certain the rest of the world was saying the same. There had perhaps been desperation too, for she sometimes thought she would be completely lost if she remained in London much longer. It was too hectic, too amoral, too cynical and superficial for one to be anything but the same.

But now a new dimension had been added to the equation. Against every measure of her expectation she found herself liking the annoying Scot. He seemed wholly free of London's taint. In fact, it was no wonder he had seemed so different from the first, for she began to suspect he was a real man, and not merely some painted fop or mincing tulip, which was all she was used to.

It was undoubtedly ironic, then, that he saw her beauty and dismissed it as being of as little importance as she knew it to be. Today he had looked at her with tolerance, which was an improvement, but no adoration; and at the back of his very blue eyes there remained a certain distaste, as if he saw into her soul and found it clearly wanting.

That was bad enough, but she was beginning to suspect

that he had so profoundly angered her because it was what she had come to fear herself.

She still had every intention of making him change his mind. His eyes would hold admiration when he looked on her, not a vague, troubling disappointment, as if she were somehow less than he expected and hoped for. If nothing else, he should be made to pay for making her feel cheap.

But she was beginning to wonder if he might not be the answer she had been looking for. He lived far away from London, he had responsibilities and a purpose in life, and it seemed to her that everyone she knew was lacking in both. She was a little surprised to discover that she had almost forgotten the wager with Harry. That had not been what had motivated her for a long time now, and it seemed a hundred years away, as if it had happened to another person.

She knew the world would think she was mad even to contemplate so uneven a match—her brothers in particular. Wedding a penniless Scot when she had jilted two of the biggest prizes on the matrimonial mart, and might have had a duke for the lifting of a finger, would shock even those inured to her starts.

But it was growing more and more tempting. To leave her old life and reputation behind—to find some worthwhile purpose—to escape from the tainted gaiety of London, seemed suddenly infinitely desirable to her.

The problem was, she had not snared her penniless Scot yet. In fact, though he had shown himself far more human at their last meeting, which was at least encouraging, she still had no indication that he thought her anything more than a spoilt and worthless beauty.

That was oddly lowering. She had never before doubted her own attractions, but then, she had never seriously pursued anyone either. It would be galling indeed to discover she could not attach the one man she wished to.

The ball seemed suddenly unbearable, the heat intense, the company intolerably insipid. Her head ached and she longed to escape, but it occurred to her unpleasantly that if she were to leave early, GlenRoss might come to hear of it, and she had no wish to thus minister to his vanity. For all her reputation, she had never before hunted in earnest, and she knew it would be fatal if GlenRoss were ever to guess her intentions.

She therefore encouraged Lavisse to engage in an increasingly public flirtation, and did not reach home until the early hours of the morning. If GlenRoss came to hear of the evening, it would be only that Lady Drewe Carlisle enjoyed herself as usual, and had not deigned to notice the absence of one insignificant Scottish peer.

Alone in her bedchamber at last, at a very late hour, she wearily dismissed her sleepy maid and sat before her dressing table regarding her reflection. She could find no trace of the beauty everyone else seemed to find there. She looked tired and discontented, with lines she did not recognize around her mouth, and violet shadows under her eyes.

Is this the way she would look when she was old and raddled? No beauty left, but still clinging to the pitiful illusion? After having drunk too much and slept too little for too many years, ruining her complexion with paint as the natural color left, in an attempt to restore what she herself had squandered so ruthlessly?

The thought frightened her, and with a sudden gesture of loathing she jerked out the absurd feathers from her hair and flung them across the floor. God, was that what she was fated to? She could not bear to look at herself any longer, and so turned hastily away. Rashly she measured out the drops that helped her sleep, for she habitually stayed up too late and rose too early, and frequently suffered from bad dreams. But tonight she had no wish to dream.

It occurred to her that she must not fail. GlenRoss seemed perhaps her last hope.

6

As the month of November drew to a close, Drewe had to acknowledge bitterly that she was making no progress with her wager. Her quarry seemed remarkably immune to her famous attractions, and though he had thawed slightly of late, it did not seem to portend any noticeable melting toward her.

Hunting now in earnest, Drewe had to acknowledge that she had mishandled the affair from the beginning. If she had meant to snare him, she should have played a more demure role, for it was clear he disapproved of her. It was too late for that now, of course. Nor did it sit at all well with her. She was determined to make him accept her as she was.

But she seemed no nearer to snaring her elusive prize. Indeed, GlenRoss seemed to blow remarkably hot and cold. Sometimes when they met he would seem to find lazy amusement in her presence, and at others he would let half an evening go by before acknowledging her. He seemed as wily as the Scots deer in his native land, and about as tamable.

In fact, the suspicion again rose that he was playing some disreputable game of his own with her. Could he have somehow guessed her intent and be deriving great enjoyment in thwarting her?

But no. It was too improbable. He could not guess—how could he?—that the great Lady Drewe Carlisle had made a wager with her brother to bring the barbarian Scot to her feet.

But that he was equally determined not to find himself at

those same feet was more than obvious. It was both ironic and maddening, for she did not know how to break down his defenses against her. Nor was it in the least flattering that Drewe had no notion whether she appealed in any way to the man she had chosen out of all others to honor with her interest.

Harry, of course, was wholly enjoying her discomfiture. He annoyed her incessantly with reminders of the rapid approach of her deadline, and took great pleasure in reporting that Lord GlenRoss had lately developed a friendship with a Miss Gaffney, the only daughter and heiress of a rich India merchant. According to Harry, the betting in the clubs was on a match being struck of mutual advantage to both parties. GlenRoss would get the financing he needed and Miss Gaffney, of undoubtedly humble stock, would buy herself a title, even if it were merely Scottish.

Drewe turned a coldly indifferent shoulder to these predictions; but she was by no means as indifferent as she would have liked Harry to believe. It seemed to her that such a match was entirely possible, and it galled her even more to have to weigh her possible advantages against those of a Miss Gaffney. Drewe had her own fortune, once she was married, but it was unlikely to finance the schemes GlenRoss had in mind. And neither her birth nor her social standing, which she had taken so carelessly for granted, nor even her beauty, was likely to count for much in the wilds of Scotland.

She was more annoyed than anything by the fact she had foolishly set herself up to allow Harry to pass judgment on her. She therefore pretended to have dismissed the absurd wager from her mind and deliberately encouraged a hot flirtation with the French *comte*. It was doubtful if Harry was fooled, however, and she could have cursed her stupidity in placing herself in such an untenable position.

Worse was to come. She was obliged to meet Miss Gaffney

in GlenRoss's company, and even under Harry's unpleasant eagle eye. She had gone to a cursedly dull card party, and was already longing to go home, when Lord GlenRoss walked in with a mousy brunette on his arm.

She was passably good-looking, with a quiet manner, and dressed overelaborately with a great many jewels and ribbons to her gown. Her figure was nothing much to speak of, and her complexion poor, but as an heiress she could easily figure as a handsome girl.

Harry happened to be standing near his sister, and soon took the opportunity to whisper maliciously in her ear, "Not bad for seventy thousand pounds, eh? She lacks your looks, my pet, but then, one can't have everything. Really, I may try to cut him out myself. They say the father is vulgar as bedamned, but I suspect my need is even greater than GlenRoss's, if possible. In fact, he's stolen a march on all of us."

Drewe turned an indifferent shoulder to this, but she could not repress a pang at the assiduous attention GlenRoss was showing his guest, in contrast to the mocking raillery he always showed toward her. He bent his head courteously to listen to what she said, supplied her with a glass of ratafia, and remained attentively by her side.

Drewe, piqued, threw herself into the play, and crowned the evening by losing one of her favorite brooches. She could have sworn with frustration, especially since it was Lavisse who won it from her. He was growing extremely demanding in his attentions, and she feared she would have to dismiss him soon. It annoyed her particularly that he should have won one of her jewels, and to have tucked it away so pointedly, an intimate little smile on his face as he did so.

It was but par for the evening that GlenRoss should have been close enough to overhear the whole.

Later Lavisse was at her side, making extravagant love

to her in a way that had long since begun to grate on her nerves, when Drewe looked up to find GlenRoss beside her, Miss Gaffney on his arm.

She had no wish for the introduction, but shook hands with the mousy heiress, saying briefly, in her distinctive voice, "How do you do? Are you enjoying the evening?"

"Oh, yes," murmured Miss Gaffney. "So kind. I wonder . . . I mean . . . I'm afraid I didn't quite catch the name. Did Lord GlenRoss say you are Lady *Drewe* Carlisle?"

"Yes, why?" asked Drewe in some surprise.

"Oh, nothing, only that my cousin—I feel sure you won't remember him—but he is a great admirer of yours," said the heiress warmly.

It was absurd. "Really?" drawled Drewe, longing for an excuse to escape. "May I make known to you the Comte de Lavisse, recently from Paris? Miss Gaffney, Lord GlenRoss."

Miss Gaffney acknowledged the introduction, but returned to what was apparently of uppermost interest to her. "My cousin will be quite overcome when I tell him I've met you, my lady."

Drewe saw GlenRoss's eyes on her in some mockery, and lifted her chin. "Really? And what is it he finds to admire in me?" she demanded abruptly.

Miss Gaffney opened her mouth. "Why . . . why . . ."

Drewe glanced again at GlenRoss. "I feel certain Lord GlenRoss would tell you that you should reserve one's admiration for someone who actually does something," she said mockingly. "I do nothing, I'm afraid."

There was reluctant acknowledgment in GlenRoss's eyes, and a certain amusement, but he said merely, "I would not presume to be so rude, I assure you."

"Wouldn't you? But you do dislike spoilt London beauties, don't you?" pursued Drewe inexorably.

He choked, but Lavisse protested, shocked. "But no! You wrong yourself, *ma cherie*. You have no need to do more than exist. Merely to observe you is enough for most of us."

"Precisely," agreed GlenRoss, his lips twitching.

Drewe would have liked to throw one of the elaborate ices that decorated the buffet in his face. She had to be content with chatting politely with Miss Gaffney, and escaping as soon as she decently could.

But seeing Miss Gaffney in GlenRoss's company had brought the rumors home to her, and she was reluctantly forced to acknowledge that her time was running out. To have to admit defeat to the daughter of an Indian merchant might be galling in the extreme, but she seemed to be making no headway in her pursuit. GlenRoss was no nearer to falling at her feet than he had ever been.

Then fate again played into her hands by making them fellow guests at a party in the country.

Drewe had willingly accepted an invitation to spend a week in Leicestershire for the hunting, even knowing that her time was running out. For one thing, she was glad to escape from her brother and his annoying gloating; and for another, she was growing weary of her unavailing quest. GlenRoss was eluding her, and it seemed there was nothing she could do about it.

The first few days in the country passed uneventfully, the ground being too wet to hunt and thus the time was spent in the usual tedious fashion of all such parties. She knew everyone present, and was bored by most, but at least Lavisse had not been invited, and both of her brothers were back in London.

But when she went down to dinner on the third night, it was to find GlenRoss with the assembled gentlemen in the hall.

She started at sight of him, and felt a blush staining her

cheeks, which was ridiculous. She took a hold on herself and came on down the stairs, scarcely able to believe her good fortune.

GlenRoss, for his part, did not seem at all surprised to see her. He waited a moment, during the general greetings, then quietly made his way to her side. "Lady Drewe."

She had herself well in hand by then. "Lord GlenRoss. This is a surprise. I would have thought hunting was yet another of those frivolous things you didn't do."

He grinned appreciably. "It's true we Scots are far more concerned with putting meat on the table than with mere sport, in the usual way, but we've a taste for it now and again. I'm told that to hunt with the Quorn is the ambition of every sporting Englishman."

"I fear you will find it vastly tame by comparison, however. It can hardly compare with . . . er . . . reiving cattle, I believe."

He laughed. "I need hardly express surprise that you hunt. Contrary to what you said the other evening, I understand you do most things superbly."

She felt the betraying warmth invade her cheeks again, and was furious with herself and with him. "I begin to think you have been too long in England, my lord," she drawled. "You are starting to learn how to flatter without saying anything, which I had come to think of as a peculiarly English trait. It would be a shame if you took that back with you."

She went on past him in to dinner without another look.

She saw little more of him that night, for he was seated at some distance from her at dinner. She was left to brood for the rest of the evening over what perversity in her nature drove her to estrange him, when the exact opposite was her goal. It would seem she was her own worst enemy.

She did not immediately see GlenRoss when they set out early the following morning. The morning was cold but dry, and she looked forward to the day. She had not had a good run for weeks, and she was interested to see how GlenRoss would acquit himself. She was herself attired in a striking new habit of deepest crimson, with a daring hat upon her streaked locks that looked like nothing so much as a man's tall beaver. Only a crimson plume curling down beside her cheek rescued it, and she knew herself to be both looking her best and to have shocked a few of the more conventional guests.

They had a good early run, as she had expected. It was sometime later in the morning when she first caught sight of GlenRoss, on the same rattail gray, as they thundered across the field.

She glanced assessingly at him, seeing that his style in the saddle was nothing to complain of now. He kept pace with her easily, and looked, in fact, more at home than a great many other men on the hunt that day. He rode with the easy grace that seemed almost a slouch but that would effortlessly eat up the miles, she well knew. Even the rattail gray had transformed himself, and looked as if he were completely tireless. She thought that so might his ancestors have looked as they rode across the glens on quick pony raids, or into battle, and the notion was a revelation to her.

She herself was looking far from her elegant self by then. The wind had stung her cheeks with hectic color and whipped her hair into a tangle. Mud liberally splashed her habit and boots, and there was a long stain of green on one cheek from a brush with a low-hanging branch.

He grinned at her as he saw her turn her head, and raised his whip in salute. For a long moment they rode side by side in unexpected companionship. Then an uproar broke out among the pack, and the odd interlude was over.

It seemed the fox had gone to earth, and they came to a halt, milling around while the scent was cast for. Drewe was breathless but exhilarated, and took the moment to unkink her shoulders and stretch her spine. Then they were off again, in full cry.

They came to a fork, and the pack split, most going across country but a few heading straight for a high wall. She hesitated only an instant, and set her black at the wall. As she cleared it she heard hoofbeats and again looked around to find GlenRoss at her heels.

Some devil made her instantly slash at her black, determined not to be overtaken by him. She would beat him in this, if nothing else, if it were the last thing she did.

For an instant she wondered if he had accepted the challenge. Then above her own she caught the satisfactory echo of thundering hooves in pursuit and smiled in triumph. He should learn yet that Lady Drewe Carlisle was not to be dismissed so lightly.

Her black was no longer fresh, but like her he responded to an outright challenge, and threw himself into the race. She had forgotten the hunt by then, forgotten all but the pursuing horse and rider, and scarcely noticed that they had left the others far behind.

For some minutes she had it all her own way, and nothing she had yet seen of GlenRoss's gray encouraged her to think him any threat. Then, to her astonishment, out of the corner of her eye she became aware of an ugly gray head doggedly gaining on her. She swore and redoubled her efforts, bending low over the black's neck and urging him on.

She exulted when the creeping gray head fell back slightly. But the next minute it had crept up again, steadily gaining on her. She swore again, and caught a glimpse of GlenRoss's face. To her fury, he seemed unmoved by the contest between them, as relaxed in the saddle as before.

Then he shouted something, lost on the wind, and pulled back slightly. She glanced ahead to see an ancient wall rapidly coming up. It was crumbling slightly and bramble-covered, but she knew her black could easily clear it.

When she glanced back, though, GlenRoss had pulled up even more, and was dropping behind, still shouting to her.

She smiled, knowing she had him, and deliberately set her black at the wall.

He took it gallantly, and cleared it with ease. But the ground on the other side fell abruptly away, and was strewn with fallen stones from the wall. Too late she realized the danger and swore as the ground came up to meet them.

There was a confused instant when she was aware of the black scrambling for a foothold. Then they were both down, falling heavily. She instinctively kicked her foot free of the stirrup and rolled, but she must have fetched up against something massive and extremely hard, for the breath was knocked completely out of her.

7

For a long moment Drewe could do no more than lie there stunned. Then a face loomed over her and GlenRoss demanded anxiously, "Are you all right?"

It took a moment for her to find her voice, and then she said weakly, "Yes, of course. See to my horse!"

His face changed and he sat back on his heels. "Then you deserved to break your beautiful, selfish little neck," he said frankly. "Didn't you hear me shouting a warning to you?"

She was becoming aware of a number of sore spots, and her breathing was still extremely shallow. But she was far more concerned about her mount. "D'you think I care for other people's warnings?" she demanded furiously. "Now, see to my black, damn you!"

He looked torn between annoyance and amusement, but after a moment shrugged and did as she bade.

By the time she had regained her feet, shaken and bruised, she was relieved to see her black also on his feet. Her heart did a funny revolt and for a weak moment faintness threatened to overcome her, for despite her words, she would never have forgiven herself if the black had suffered any serious hurt.

But she would not give GlenRoss the satisfaction of knowing that, and so fought back the shameful weakness. "Is he all right?" she demanded gruffly.

GlenRoss glanced up from where he knelt inspecting the black's right fore. "No thanks to you," he said bluntly. "He's broken the skin and there's some swelling, but I think no permanent damage has been done. You're lucky this time."

She ignored that, though her heart was still doing funny things in her breast and it was necessary to blink back unexpected tears. "Never mind that. We must get him back to my groom immediately. He'll know what to do."

He glanced at her again, making her aware for the first time of what she must look like. Her habit was torn and dirty, she had lost her cocky little hat, and her tawny hair was tumbled down her back like a slattern's.

He said more gently, "You're in no state yet to ride back. Sit down, for God's sake, before you fall down."

She lifted her chin. "That was not a request, my lord," she said dangerously. "If you don't care to accompany me, you may remain here."

He eyed her calmly once more, as if she were some rare creature who had never come to his attention before, and one that he did not much care for. Then he shrugged and rose to his feet. "Has anyone ever told you you are a damned nuisance?" he inquired pleasantly, and strode off.

She turned in astonishment, for she had not really expected him to abandon her. But in a moment he returned, carrying a handful of some deep moss or other. "This will effectively bring down the swelling until we can get back. Hold this while I remove my neckcloth. I need something to fasten it on with."

She looked extremely skeptical, but immediately whipped off her own stock. "Use this instead. My habit's ruined anyway."

His brows rose at her tone, which was peremptory. But

after a moment he shrugged and bent to bind an efficient-looking poultice with it around the black's rapidly swelling knee.

"Where did you learn to do that?" she asked grudgingly.

"Necessity. We've seldom a nice snug stable at our disposal, as you have here. We've learned to make do with what we can find. Now, let's see to you."

"Do you mean to use such home remedies on me as well?" she demanded in amusement.

He grinned. "I'm tempted, I'll confess. But that was a bruising fall you took. At the very least your head must be rattling."

"I'm used to falls," she said indifferently.

"That, at least, I can believe. Have you no sense, you little fool?"

She did not relish this form of address, and so bridled immediately. He saw it, and added annoyingly, "No, no, I know you've the devil's own temper, but you should know by now you'll not succeed in coming to cuffs with me, so don't try it. The main thing is to get you back. Do you think you're up to being thrown up on my Rufus?"

He seemed to be treating her as a recalcitrant child, which she was far from appreciating. Nor did she look with favor upon the points of his rangy gray. "I'd rather walk," she said truthfully.

"Aye, but I'd like to get back sometime today, if it's all the same to you. And unless I much mistake the matter, we're in for a storm," GlenRoss pointed out in amusement.

She glanced up, annoyed to see he was right. "If you are afraid of a little rain, then go back on your own by all means," she taunted him. "I don't need you."

The words were scarcely out of her mouth when it began to drizzle. She was so bedraggled already that it scarcely mattered to her, but he hesitated only a moment. Before she could guess his intention, he had taken the reins from her hands and lifted her bodily into his saddle.

She seldom relished being manhandled, and she was already furious at being caught in such a ridiculous position. She would have struck out at him had he not stepped quickly out of range. "Oh, no you don't," he said, still in amusement. "We can fight it out later, you little hellcat. But I'm damned if I'm going to soak myself merely to suit your pride. It's yet another Scots idiosyncrasy! There's a barn of sorts not far behind us. We can take shelter there until the rain lets up."

He immediately began to lead both horses, and since the rain had indeed grown heavier, she sat there fuming and allowed it. Even to her it seemed ridiculous to stand in the rain disputing it. But she would not soon forget his high-handedness. No one had ever dared to treat her so before, and he would very soon learn to regret it.

It was not far to the barn, as he had said, but they were both soaked to the skin by the time they reached it.

It proved to be a dilapidated structure with an earthen floor, enclosed only on three sides, but there was a rick of hay at one end, and they could at least find shelter from the storm. Drewe dismounted quickly, before he could come to lift her down, and began to unfasten the saddle.

"I'll do that," he said peremptorily. "Go on in and get out of the rain!"

She ignored him. "This cold is doing neither of them any good," she snapped, bending to pick up a handful of straw. "See to my black."

After a moment he shrugged and followed her example, removing the black's saddle and beginning to rub him down, whistling cheerfully under his breath. A moment later and he went to fetch hay for both animals. He checked the bandage again on the black's leg, satisfying himself it was still in place, and said finally, "Now we'll see to our own comfort. A fire will undoubtedly smoke the place up a bit, but under the circumstances I hope you've no objection to that."

She stood, reluctantly impressed, as he busied himself once more, gathering more straw for kindling, and a motley collection of odd sticks and lumber that looked reasonably dry. He was extremely annoying, but she had to admit that few men of her acquaintance would have been as useful in a similar circumstance. He was still whistling cheerfully between his teeth, and at last knelt to light his odd fire, patiently nursing sparks from his tinderbox in the dry straw until a thin stream of smoke rose curling from the center.

"Where did you learn to do that?" she demanded grudgingly.

He grinned. "Most Scotsmen and many a Scotswoman of my acquaintance have spent more of their time in the open than otherwise. And since we're particular about our comfort, we've learned to build a fire out of almost anything. With a cozy fire and a plaid to wrap oneself in, there's little else we ask for."

She was again curious despite herself when he spoke of what seemed another world. "You don't wear a plaid, as you call it," she pointed out.

He glanced up briefly from his work. "No. That would indeed make me a figure of fun in London, for you Southerners lack the proper respect for so useful a garment. And I fear we've all lost the habit of wearing one, since the privilege was just restored to us some dozen years ago."

"Just restored to you?" she asked in astonishment, coming to stand over the small but steadily growing flame. She hated to admit it, but a fire would indeed be welcome.

He glanced at her again, without expression, and went to fetch her a box that would serve as a stool. "It's not a Louis

Quinze chair, I regret, milady," he said, bowing extravagantly. "But it should be more comfortable than sitting on the ground."

"Good God, I'm not made of Dresden!" she complained. "I don't melt in a little rain or catch my death from a touch of cold."

He looked amused again. "So I'm beginning to see. But no Scot invites discomfort if he can avoid it. We've enough of that as it is. Take off your coat and we'll dry it before the fire."

She reluctantly did as he bade, for it was indeed clammy and miserable by now. He took it from her and improvised a stick to hang it from. And since her teeth were beginning to chatter, she sat unwillingly down on the box and huddled before the fire.

He grinned at this capitulation and added, "I regret I'm no lady's maid, but I can remove your boots for you. They must be as sodden as mine are."

She longed to refuse, not out of modesty, but pique. But the idea that he expected her to do just that, and the reminder of her frozen toes, made her at last languidly extend a booted foot for his ministrations.

He clasped one muddy boot and drew it off gently, then the other. "You'd make a tolerable lady's maid," she conceded.

He seemed untouched by the faint gibe in her tone. "Oh, aye, I'm a dab hand at most things I set my mind to," he acknowledged cheerfully. "And I've three sisters, so I'm not without experience. It's a shame I've no meal to offer you. I could show you what a Scot can do with a fire and some game to make a meal fit for a king."

"Are all Scotsmen as vain as you?" she demanded.

"Oh, aye. We're a vain race." He grinned. "Almost as bad as the English."

She ignored that. "I'm not hungry, but I confess I am devilishly thirsty. Do your powers extend to conjuring up tea as well as fire?"

"I regret I came ill-prepared, counting myself in tame England and unlikely to meet with an emergency," he conceded. "But let me see what I can do."

Before she could prevent him, he had shouldered on his wet coat again and disappeared into the rain. She shrugged and stretched her hands to the growing blaze, acknowledging that he was as unpredictable as he was annoying. And that was by no means all bad, for most men of her acquaintance were wearily predictable.

He reappeared after a few minutes, soaked again and carrying his hat lined with a handkerchief and filled to the brim with water.

"It's unconventional, I'll grant you, but beggars can't be choosers. My lady." He went elaborately on one knee and offered the water to her, his tongue firmly in cheek.

She ignored that and drank thirstily, using her hands to cup it to her mouth.

She then sat back, despite herself beginning to be filled with an unfamiliar sense of contentment, and began to run her fingers through her tangled hair. "You haven't a comb, by any chance, have you?" she asked mockingly. "Perhaps you could carve me one out of a piece of wood? You seem capable of all else."

He grinned. "Given a knife and a day or two, no doubt I could oblige you. But I warned you I came unprepared for roughing it."

She finished finger-combing her damp curls and began idly to plait it to keep it out of her way. "You said earlier that the privilege of wearing the plaid was just restored to you?" she asked curiously. "What did you mean by that?"

"Ah, and why should I be surprised you don't know about

that?'' he mused, coming to sit opposite her. He had removed his own coat and hung it on a similar branch, and looked very much at his ease. She had to admit that he looked natural there, as if indeed he spent as many hours beside a fire as indoors. "But I daresay it is indeed no more than a local tragedy, when all's said and done.''

"How can wearing or not wearing a garment be a tragedy?'' she persisted. "That sounds ridiculous.''

"Perhaps, though it was far-reaching and galling enough to those it affected. And you've not a clue what I'm speaking of, have you?'' he added humorously. "Perhaps it's good to get away, so one can see one's own troubles in perspective. I'm speaking of the 'Forty-five, of course. The late Rebellion, to you. After it was over, all Scots were forbidden to wear the traditional tartan on pain of jail or deportation. Didn't you know that? The ban was lifted only some dozen years ago.''

Her brow wrinkled in some bewilderment. "But why on earth would anyone care about that?''

"And thus speaks a Sassenach! Your leaders were wiser than you are, I'm afraid. They knew that to deny a Scotsman the right to his traditional dress is to deny him his identity—which of course is what they set out to do. If they could afford no better, Scots everywhere were forced to sew their plaids into trews and dye them with saffron. As you may have discovered by now, we're a vain people, and it little sat with our vanity, if nothing else.''

"Do you always make light of everything?'' she demanded impatiently.

He grimaced. "No. But I'll admit it is my chief failing. My sister says I've no more sensibility than a sheep, and I'm afraid she has the right of it in the main. She certainly has suffered from it often enough, I regret to say.''

"You mentioned you have three.'' She had intended to

snub him, but it occurred to her that for all his talk he had revealed very little of himself. She was curious despite herself.

"Aye, and all plaguey nuisances, I'll confess. Like most women, they think to know my business best and would love to run my life for me. Fortunately they're all away from home now, and are too busy to have my reform as their chief occupation any longer."

"Where are they?"

"Lillibet is in Edinburgh. She's the eldest and is the sister I was just speaking of. She's married now, and has three daughters of her own. Jeanne is in Glasgow, and also married. She's great with her first, and would have you believe that no one else had ever borne a bairn before. Margaret, the youngest, is away at school there and living with her."

He spoke affectionately, and she knew an unexpected pang. She had never known what it was like to have a family that was close like that. "And do you have any brothers?" she asked quickly.

A shadow seemed to cross his open face, which surprised her. Then he shrugged. "I've one, who's the youngest of us all, and the most impertinent. He's away also at school, in France, and I confess I miss his disrespectful grin."

"In France?" she repeated, astonished.

"Oh, aye. Did you think we were indeed barbarians? I'll admit we've excellent universities both in Edinburgh and Glasgow, among the oldest in Europe. But don't forget the Auld Alliance. France and Scotland have been united for centuries, largely in hatred of the English, and we've a history of sending our sons abroad to school. I myself was educated in Paris, and greatly enjoyed it." Again he sobered. "Though from what I hear from Robbie, it's much changed since I was last there."

She was indeed surprised, and found her image of him suddenly altering. She had given it little thought, but it seemed the popular English view of the barbarous Scots had infected her more than she knew.

After a moment he drew himself from his musing and said, "But that's more than enough about me. What of your own family? You've two brothers, I understand."

She laughed without humor. "Yes, I've two brothers. But we share little more than common blood. Graydon is frankly a devil, and Charlie, though I like him better, is almost as bad. Neither, I assure you, would trouble to speak so affectionately of me as you have done of your sisters."

His brows rose. "I'm sure you're mistaken. Considering the tricks we've played on one another, I doubt but that my sisters would say the same. But we've a fondness for each other, for all that."

"Have you? I'm afraid we've little liking, let alone fondness for each other. As for tricks, my brothers once took me out at night and left me to make my own way home. I was ten at the time, and no doubt a cursed nuisance. But I've never forgotten it—or forgiven them. We are not, you see, a particularly close family," she added with derision.

After a moment he asked quietly, "And your father? Lord Wrexham?"

Her beautiful mouth twisted. "Harry merely follows in his footsteps. My father is not as malicious, but quite as self-centered. As are we all. Everything you've heard of us is true. We are all of us devils. But then, you knew that already. You've disapproved of me from the first moment we met."

Again he hesitated. Then he shrugged. "Oh, I don't know. When you trouble to forget your airs and graces, you're not so bad."

This to the most accredited beauty in London! "My God,"

she cried, torn between amusement and anger. "You are devilishly blunt!"

He grinned. "But then, I'm naught but a barbarous Scot. But if you'd troubled to show this side to me earlier, instead of the imperious beauty, I might have been in some danger of falling victim to your lures, I'll confess."

She stiffened, every faculty suddenly on the alert. "You . . . you . . . How dare you! You are certainly conceited beyond all permission!"

"Oh, aye, I'm vain enough, I'll admit," he conceded peaceably. "But far from blind—or stupid. You had a bet on with your brothers that you could bring me to your feet. Did you really think I wouldn't guess?"

8

For a moment she was stunned. Then she was on her feet. "How long have you known, damn you?"

He grinned up at her. "Almost from the beginning, I should imagine. You're too accustomed to your spineless English court, I fear. In Scotland we've more pride than to slaver before an imperious beauty with little heart and still less conscience."

"Harry!" she cried furiously. "I might have known."

"No, it was not your brother. Good God, you English obviously think all Scots are beneath contempt, but did you really imagine me so vain I would believe you showed me such distinguished favor for the sake of my *beaux yeux*? I had been in London scarcely a few days before I heard of your reputation, my lady. And I have been more than amused watching you try to swallow that abominable temper of yours enough to attach me."

Drewe had been called many things in her brief career, including goddess and Aphrodite; but she had never before been called amusing. She gasped. "You . . . you . . . !"

"Impertinent barbarian?" he offered helpfully. It was clear he was making a valiant effort not to laugh. "Encroaching Scots burr? You are not usually so slow-witted."

"Yes, all of those!" she flared back. "You deliberately led me on to make a fool of myself, damn you!"

He was losing his battle not to laugh. "Aye, but it wasn't

very hard, you must admit. I will confess I wondered why you'd accepted such a wager, for it seems you've little knack for being conciliating, lass. However much you tried to attach me, your temper kept breaking through to spoil it.''

"You . . . you . . ."

"Never mind," he said kindly. "I will admit I've too much vanity to wish to have my scalp added to any woman's belt, no matter how beautiful or imperious. But in the main I've hugely enjoyed it. You enlivened a generally tedious stay for me, and I thank you for it. I return to Scotland at the end of the week, so you've no need to see my annoying face any longer."

He too had risen and now held out his hand, saying winningly, "Come, I hope we can cry friends. No hard feelings?"

Drewe had undergone a flood of emotions, few of them in any way gratifying. Anger, annoyance, shame—all drove her to fury. But above all was a curious blankness, brought about by the news that he was returning to Scotland.

But she had no intention of showing herself to even worse advantage than she had already, and so she took his hand, saying in her forthright way, "At least I know when I've been fairly beaten."

"That's generous of you. But I should say we are about even."

The next moment she had pulled him strongly forward, catching him off-guard, and neatly threw him over her hip. It was a trick Charlie had once taught her, and it stood her in excellent stead now. GlenRoss went crashing over her to land headfirst in the hayrick behind her.

For a moment there was a stunned silence, and she turned quickly to see him flat on his back in the hay, his clothes and hair generously decorated with straw, looking exceedingly foolish.

She couldn't help it. She burst out laughing. "You were mistaken. *Now* we are even!" she announced triumphantly.

To do him credit, he accepted it in very good spirit, merely lying there grinning up at her. "Very funny. Where'd you learn such a trick?"

"From my brother Charlie. He thought it might come in useful sometime. It seems he was right."

"I must remember to teach it to my sisters." He sat up and winced. "On second thought, their husbands would never forgive me. You make a considerable impression, lass. But mayhap I deserved it." He shook the straw from his hair and rose to his knees.

"You did, if for no other reason than your unbearably sanctimonious air," she said positively. "You speak a good deal of the Scots, but if they are all as vain and conceited as you, it is no wonder they have been ill-treated. We English may not be perfect, but we at least have the advantage of good manners."

He grinned and rubbed his back. "Oh, aye, you're a tediously polite race, even when you are cracking the whip over other people's heads. But we've less facility for smiling betrayal, I fear."

Without warning he abruptly lunged forward and grasped her ankle. It had not occurred to her that he might retaliate, but she saw instantly that it should have. He was indeed a barbarian, and no gentleman, for he ruthlessly jerked her feet out from under her, tumbling her heavily on top of him in the hay.

For a moment she was too stunned to react. Then she pulled herself up and struck at his grinning face, meaning to wipe the grin away once and for all.

Once again he was too fast for her. He caught her wrist in a painful grip and restrained her with unexpected strength.

"Oh, no, you little vixen," he said, still annoyingly

amused. "If your English admirers are in the habit of letting you strike them, they've less spirit even than we usually allow them—and that's little enough. God knows."

Her temper was seldom governable, and she could not remember the last time she had been in such a rage. "You . . . Confound you!" she cried, attempting to pry her wrist free. "How *dare* you! You are clearly no gentleman."

"Aye, now you begin to understand," he said in amusement, making no attempt to release her. "And in that case, it should be a fairly equal match between us."

He was being generous, however. She was ignominiously sprawled half on top of him, and quickly discovered her strength was no match for his own. He held her easily, and added cheerfully, "But it does occur to me I have been less than gentlemanly, my lady. After all, I had it dinned into my thick head from the time I was fostered that a gentleman must always give in to the fairer sex. And since you are obviously in the mood for a quarrel, I've no real objection to indulging you. I'll even give you further provocation, if you wish. After all, never let it be said a Scotsman cruelly denied a beautiful lady."

Quick as a flash he forced her over onto her back in the filthy straw and captured her other flailing wrist. He held them both above her head and clipped them together in one strong hand, rendering her struggles humiliatingly futile.

She was outraged, for she had never been so roughly treated in her life. And it was particularly galling that he forced her to confront her own weakness, for she had never before been made to acknowledge that a man was intrinsically stronger than she was and could impose his will on her whenever he chose.

Only slowly did it dawn on her that his object was to kiss her. He held her wrists immobile with one hand and pinned her legs down with one of his own. His remaining hand he used to grasp a painful handful of her tawny hair and hold her head captive.

She thought furiously that she would rather die than let him succeed. Despite the pain it caused her, she twisted her head frantically, swearing violently and with little regard for a lady's vocabulary, and renewed her struggles to release herself.

He held her easily, but she thought she detected the first hint of surprise in his eyes she had yet seen there. "Lie still, little hellion," he warned her. "You'll only succeed in bruising yourself, for you'll not get away."

She scorned to obey him. "Damn you! This may be the way you woo women in your barbaric country, but it does not work here."

"Aye, we've a habit of tossing them over our saddlebows and riding off with them when they prove recalcitrant, so be warned," he teased. "You may have found it amusing to try to bring me to your feet, but you'd find it far less amusing to be wedded to me, I promise you."

"You flatter yourself!" she cried scornfully. "I would not wed you if you were the last man on earth!"

"Aye, you lack the basic equipment," he agreed infuriatingly. "Nature made you damnably beautiful, but you've little else to boast of. When I take a wife, it will be someone who has more than a pretty face to offer."

"Like Miss Gaffney!" she retorted. "Doubtless her father's fortune is worth far more than a mere pretty face!"

He whistled. "Oho, so that's what's partly behind this, is it? I'm flattered you should be jealous, lass, but I'm no' for sale to any woman."

"Jealous!"

"No," he said thoughtfully. "To be jealous presumes you possess a heart, and I doubt that you do."

"None that you shall ever discover! Let me go, damn you!"

"In a bit. I'd no intention of going this far," he conceded, still thoughtfully. "But it seems I can't resist. And certainly it's more than time someone taught you a lesson, my lady."

"It won't be you!" she said with loathing, beginning to struggle anew.

He laughed and easily restrained her. "And that's what galls you the most, isn't it? That a mere man might be stronger than you and dare to impose his will on you. You do despise us all, don't you?"

"Yes!" she panted, winded and furious.

"I thought as much. I've watched you use your beauty as a weapon, time after time. It's no wonder you've been through two fiancés already. Once you've reduced them to jelly, you've no interest left in them at all, have you?"

"You . . . you . . . !"

"So we're back to that, are we? Come, that's not very original. Where is your famous vitriolic tongue, my lady? The truth is, you're powerless against anyone who doesn't quake at one spark from your beautiful amber eyes, aren't you? And that must be galling indeed."

"You . . . I'll . . . "

"Don't worry. I'm almost done. But I really think it would benefit you to reap what you sow for once. You drive the poor fools about you to desperation, never caring a jot yourself and enjoying seeing them squirm. And you also count on the fact none of them seems to have the courage or the bad manners to pay you back in your own coin. But I am a barbaric Scot, remember? And I've nothing to lose."

For a moment longer they confronted each other as antagonists, she panting and ruffled and furious, yet for once oddly silent; and he still faintly smiling and maddeningly cool. Then he lowered his head and with humiliating ease claimed her mouth.

She should have continued to fight him, but she would have been hypocritical indeed not to admit that underlying her anger had long since begun to appear a strange and breathless excitement. And she was nothing if not honest with herself.

Nor was he wrong that not one of her adoring court would have dared to treat her in this way. The few kisses she had so far endured had been clumsy and respectful, pressed upon her by worshipful admirers.

She had never before liked to be touched, and despite her reputation had never encouraged such familiarities. Why, then, was this violent assault somehow different? She forgot her determination to resist and closed her eyes experimentally, sampling the sensation, forgetting all else in her curiosity to explore and analyze it. Could it be that she had been wrong about lovemaking, and that there was something to it, after all?

Still experimentally, she tried relaxing her lips. Instantly the nature of his kiss changed, growing softer and yet somehow still more demanding. She made a sound deep in her throat, of surprise and pleasure, and wriggled her hands, no longer struggling against her bonds but in protest against her lack of freedom.

He let them go immediately. Somehow they had shifted so that he was not so heavily on top of her. She was free now, but quite without her own volition her arms came down to twine about his neck, straining him ever closer to her. Her lips had long since parted, and her first intent at experimentation had become no more than a hazy memory in her mind. But she found that kissing cut off one's wind shockingly, for why else should she be so light-headed?

As if reading her mind, GlenRoss abandoned her mouth

and buried his face in her throat. Her fine cambric shirt was open at the neck and still uncomfortably damp, but everywhere his lips touched turned somehow to flame. She gasped for breath, cold and yet hot at the same time, wondering why no one had ever shown her this before. Could it really be that other people had experienced these sensations before, and this mind-destroying paralysis? If so, it was a monstrous deception, for no one had ever told her.

GlenRoss, too, seemed momentarily to have lost all mockery. His hands cradled her head, fitting her mouth again to his own with a kind of subdued violence. But for all his barbarity, his hands were oddly gentle, adoring her in a way that none of her adoring court seemed capable of. He murmured feverishly too, as if against his will, as he kissed her. "Aye, that's it, lass. You've a mighty sweet mouth, for all your vitriol."

One of the horses, neighing shrilly, at last brought them to their senses. GlenRoss reluctantly raised his head, and for a long moment Drewe lay there, her eyes closed, too spent to think or protest, and liking the sensation for once in her life.

Then GlenRoss shattered the brief idyll.

"Who'd have thought it?" he mused, watching her with half-closed eyes. "For all her reputation, the Lady Drewe Carlisle betrays a shocking inexperience at lovemaking. I begin to think we were always right, and all English are unforgivably clumsy. But you're a fast learner, lass, I'll give you that. And sweeter than you've any right to be."

Instantly her eyes opened and she stiffened, remembering far too late all that lay between them. "Damn you! You know nothing of me."

He laughed lazily and brushed her tawny hair back from her face. "I know a great deal more than I did, you must confess," he observed smugly, his eyes running possessively over her swollen mouth and flushed face. He laughed again, quite obviously pleased with himself. "You make me almost sorry I won't be the one to complete your education."

Furiously she thrust him off and sat up, rearranging her clothes and pawing the straw from her hair. "You . . . you . . ."

"Ah, we're back to that, are we?" he asked in amusement, sitting up himself. "But stimulating as this conversation is, it has ceased to rain, in case you hadn't noticed. We should be getting back before they send out a rescue party. That might indeed prove embarrassing, under the circumstances."

"Get out! I would rather die than ride another step with you! No. I would far rather kill you, and I may if you don't get away from me!"

"Don't forget, you started this, sweetheart," he rejoined, still grinning. "It was not quite the lesson I meant to teach you, but I suspect it will suffice. Remember this the next time you think to ensnare a man for the amusement of it, or play off your tricks and expect not to get burnt. Some men are not as cowed as others, and are apt to turn violent in turn. I suspect you've been lucky until now, but that luck was certain to run out. Be thankful it was with me, and you emerged relatively unscathed. For you were at far more risk than I think you know just now. And you'd no mind to stop it either."

"*Damn* you!" she cried again, panting in her rage. "You flatter yourself!"

"Do I? I don't think so. You've learned something of the power of passion, and that can't be all bad either. In fact, I think you should be grateful to me. All men are not painted weaklings, and passion in the end means very little, as you've just discovered."

She groped about her for some punishment bad enough,

and in the end was reduced to grabbing up one of her boots and slinging it at his head.

He effortlessly ducked, and rose, still laughing. "Aye, I'm going. We Scots have many faults, but we've an excellent sense of self-preservation. I'll send a party back to find you. And since I doubt we'll meet again, I'll bid you farewell. It's been . . . interesting, at the very least. I'll not soon forget you, if that's any consolation."

Still chuckling, he saddled up his horse, shrugged on his still-wet jacket, and in another moment was gone.

Lady Drewe Carlisle, left for the first time in her life to contemplate the folly of her own actions, threw herself on the ground in a paroxysm of fury and beat futilely against the straw, wishing it was GlenRoss's smiling face.

9

True to his word, GlenRoss left England at the end of the week.

Drewe had no intention of sharing with her brothers that final humiliating scene, but it was inevitable they should quickly learn of GlenRoss's return to Scotland. Harry was insufferable, even after she grudgingly handed over her emeralds to him.

"Rumor has it he reached an agreement with the nabob's daughter, in fact," he said maliciously. "I fear you are eclipsed, my pet. Really, I have not enjoyed myself so much in I don't know when."

That was bad enough, but whatever face she was careful to show Harry, she was conscious of having suffered a decided blow, if only to her pride. It was indeed something to be eclipsed by a Miss Gaffney, even without everything else that had gone between them. Confound Harry for luring her into such a wager in the first place.

As for GlenRoss, the man was a fool—a barbarian!—and for a while she nursed some unworthy thoughts of revenge. He was fortunate to be in his distant Highlands. Her only comfort was that she had had the forethought to set up a flirtation with Lavisse. Harry should at least never guess how badly she had been spurned, and how much it rankled.

But there was something else the Scotsman had left her, for despite herself, not all her memories were equally unpleasant. Even that last humiliating scene had had its moments, for in half an hour he had taught her more of passion than she had ever known before.

That rankled too, since it would seem he had emerged unscathed. For all her reputation, Drewe generally disliked being touched. Those of her admirers bold enough to try to kiss her had usually contented themselves with her hand or cheek or a chaste salute on the lips. Even both her fiancés had not progressed much further, for she had always thought lovemaking faintly distasteful, and held them at a distance as only she knew how to do.

Well, GlenRoss had shown her she had been mistaken. But since he lacked both finesse and polish, and had treated her roughly into the bargain, she scorned to admit that what she had experienced with him was in any way unique, and set out to prove it.

Lavisse was as sophisticated as GlenRoss was uncouth, as suave as the Scotsman was rough, and thus a perfect choice. He also had the advantage of being somewhat older than most of her court, and undoubtedly far more experienced. More, he was as worldly as he was shrewd, and would not expect more from their flirtation than she offered. She doubted he was hanging out for a wife at all, and while he might profess his undying devotion, had no intention of offering for her.

She accordingly allowed him to escort her home one evening, and suffered him to take her into his arms.

If he was surprised, for she had consistently rebuffed any such attempts in the past, he was certainly not loath. He instantly smothered her face in impassioned kisses, crying, "Ah, my angel . . . my goddess! You do not know what you do to me!"

She thought critically that he sounded more experienced than genuinely impassioned, but instantly dismissed such an unworthy cavil. He also smelt unpleasantly of a florid scent that in the close confines of the carriage was making her feel slightly unwell. But she rigidly refused to allow such casual criticism.

She disliked having her face dabbed with kisses, though, and finally turned up her mouth, impatient with the delay. He swooped instantly in triumph, exclaiming in French. It seemed his English had escaped him in the heat of the moment.

He was undoubtedly experienced, and betrayed not the least hesitation or diffidence. His mouth tasted faintly of brandy and cigars, which was not unpleasant; and he assumed in her an experience to equal his own.

But she lay in his arms as if she were split in two, one half of her experiencing the scent and feel of his lips, which were slightly cool and unpleasantly wet; and the other half watching and measuring her reactions with complete detachment. And neither half experienced the delirious soaring release she had known in GlenRoss's arms.

It was maddening, and she sat up suddenly, with less than politic attention to Lavisse's pride. "Oh, blast it! Is that the best you can do?"

It was scarcely flattering, and Lavissa looked both surprised and a little hurt. *"Ma belle! Qu'est que c'est?"*

She recalled too late that she had invited the absurd episode, and so made some excuse of having heard a carriage approach. He did not look convinced, but tried to draw her back into his arms, murmuring that it was nothing. No one would disturb them. But even he had to soon admit that the mood had been broken and gave it up.

He made the best of it, but she could see his pride had been wounded. And that was yet another thing to chalk up to GlenRoss's account.

In fact, she was finding little joy in anything these days.

There was no one in town of interest, the social events she attended were tedious beyond compare, everything had been done and said a thousand times before. If she had been un-bearably bored before that absurd wager, she was driven to distraction now, and she could see no escape. She had tried once to alter her fate and it had ended in disaster. She was not sure she possessed the energy a second time.

Then something occurred to make all of her previous disgust of London and the life she led seem like a mere child's tantrum by comparison.

Lavisse, after the unflattering episode, had begun to show less marked attention to her, and Harry twitted her upon having lost yet another of her beaux. She shrugged scorn-fully and ignored him, but it did not occur to her that Lavisse would brag of the episode, and give it a very different coloring in the retelling, with tragic consequences.

The first inkling she had of the true state of affairs was at an afternoon reception for an Italian ambassador. She had no desire to go, expecting it to be deadly dull and, in her present mood, beyond tolerance, but Harry was keeping a sharp eye on her these days, and she would not give him the satisfaction of seeing her cry off.

As soon as she entered the room, however, she knew some-thing was wrong. Conversation seemed to break off, only to resume a moment later with a slightly strained air, and a number of covert and not-so-covert stares were cast in her direction.

She was used to being stared at and to riding out scandals, and so lifted her head and strode on into the room, refusing to notice the stares. She bade a gracious hello to her hostess, who seemed somewhat distracted, and passed on, betraying no hint of her awareness that anything was wrong.

But she was puzzled. A number of acquaintances greeted her and stayed to chat, but like their hostess, their manners seemed slightly strained. And wherever she went, low-voiced conversation came to an abrupt end and curious eyes followed her, by no means admiring.

She was growing seriously annoyed, and wondered what she could have done this time to put the world in a stir. The reception was even more tedious than she had expected, but under the circumstances she could not indulge her growing inclination and depart early. She was obligated, for the sake of her pride and to confound her critics, to remain with every semblance of enjoyment for at least an hour.

But it was not until she had retired to repair a flounce that had been carelessly trodden on that she learned the truth. And then all thoughts of her pride were abandoned.

She was returning lightly down the stairs when she heard the particularly penetrating voice of one of her worst critics, in close conversation with another woman whom Drewe had once snubbed. "As bold as brass!" she was saying in loathing. "It did not occur to me that she would have the courage to put in an appearance here, after what has happened. But then, I have always said she would dare anything! And not even a sign of experiencing any guilt! I tell you, she is completely without a heart."

Drewe stood listening, her brows raised in bewilderment and annoyance. But as the voice droned on, and its import became clear, she gasped, and forgot both that she was eavesdropping and that someone might come along.

For a long time after her two malicious critics had wandered away she clung to the banister, scarcely aware of what she did, and the party below forgotten. She felt oddly numb, and somewhat light-headed, and aware of a growing feeling of unreality.

It was not until a maid came along and stared oddly at her, asking if she were ill, that she forced herself to lift her head and make her way down the stairs. Fortunately she encountered no one but lackeys in the hall, but she was unable to bear even their curious eyes. She did not stay to retrieve her cloak or wait for her carriage to be ordered, but plunged outside, ignoring their startled exclamations.

The cold December afternoon seemed even more unreal, for it seemed like aeons had passed, not mere hours, since she had set out that morning. She turned and began to walk blindly, with no idea where she was going and wholly unaware that it had begun to snow.

Luckily she met no one she knew. She did not feel the cold; only a profound sickness that threatened even yet to leave her retching on the side of the street, and seemed to penetrate to her very soul. She drew considerable attention, for an out-and-out beauty, in the flimsiest of expensive gowns, walking without cloak or attendants, the snow clinging to her lovely tawny locks, was hardly a common sight. But though she had by then penetrated into far-from-genteel neighborhoods, the look in her eyes was such that somehow no one cared to accost her.

She had been walking for she knew not how long, and was cold to the bone, when a voice she knew well exclaimed in astonishment, "Good God! Lady Drewe?"

That halted her. She looked up vaguely, not even very surprised to see GlenRoss. Certainly all that had passed between them seemed a long time ago, and no longer of any consequence. "You . . . ?" she said vaguely. "I thought you had gone back to Scotland."

"I did," he answered briefly, concern for her white face and shaken manner evident. "Good God, what has occurred? Are you all right?"

She laughed then, a sound that was shocking even to herself. "All right? Yes, I'm all right. Excuse me. I must go."

"I think I should take you home, lass," he insisted, noting

her soaked gown and frozen look. "You're wet through."

That brought another laugh from her. "Home! What a charming word. But I'm afraid I have no home."

He glanced around, very concerned now, and held her firmly by one arm. Abruptly he hailed a hackney, and as it pulled up, shrugged out of his heavy driving coat and wrapped her in it.

She suffered herself to be bundled into the hackney because she lacked the strength to fight him. She felt as drained and weak as if she were suffering from some debilitating disease, but some part of her mind told her it was imperative that she pull herself together and not break down in front of him, of all people. "Wh-what are you d-doing here?" she demanded, her teeth beginning to chatter. "You had g-gone back to S-Scotland."

"Aye. But I had some unfinished business." He was watching her closely, concern evident on his face.

"M-Miss G-Gaffney, no doubt," she said, despising the way her body had begun to shudder—whether with cold or reaction, it was impossible to say.

"Miss Gaffney?" he repeated in astonishment.

"You are g-going to m-marry her, aren't y-you?" Pride kept her head up, but it was no doubt a false one at best. He would know soon enough of her downfall, and he would be free to despise her with the rest of the world. But then, he despised her already. Only not, it seemed, as much as she despised herself.

"Good God, no. Whatever gave you that idea?"

It seemed too great an effort to answer him. She was shuddering with the cold now, and it took all her strength not to break down in front of him. That would be the final humiliation. "P-please, just let me out," she cried desperately. "I . . . I need to be alone."

"No. Not until you tell me what's wrong, lass." He spoke

uncompromisingly, and though he did not attempt to touch her, he was very close beside her in the confines of the odorous coach.

She had an absurd desire to break out laughing again. "Wrong? What could possibly be wrong?" she managed. "Don't you know I'm Lady Drewe Carlisle? All of the Carlisles have no hearts, the whole world knows that. We use people and then throw them away. My father and brothers will indeed be proud of me today. Oh, *God*!"

Abruptly she buried her face in her hands and began to sob in a way she had not done since she was a child.

10

GlenRoss stared at her in astonishment for a moment. Then with a wry grimace he took her in his arms. "Nay, lass, it can't be as bad as all that," he murmured soothingly. "Dinna fash yourself, as Duncan would say."

"You don't know!" she sobbed like a little child.

He let her cry, soothing her as he would one of his nieces, murmuring meaningless phrases. In truth it was hard to recall that he held the beautiful Lady Drewe Carlisle in his arms, for she seemed little older than one of his nieces at the moment. Certainly she was as headstrong, passionate, and spoilt as his five-year-old niece, who would stamp her foot if she didn't get her way and ruled her world with an imperious will of iron. But his niece had already learned to thread her arms around her uncle's neck and cajole when she desired something, while Lady Drewe was as prickly and defensive as a hedgehog.

At length she quietened and lay passively in his arms. All spirit and will seemed to be drained from her, and it was a long time before she at last sat up, pushing the tumbled hair out of her eyes and rubbing her face with the palms of her hands like a child.

"Here, use this." He offered her his own handkerchief. "At the moment you look like my eldest niece, who knuckles her eyes in just such a way when she's been crying."

She took the handkerchief, too spent even to take offense

at that. "I'm sorry," she said numbly. "You must think me a complete fool."

"Nay, I think you human," he said humorously. "Here, let me. You've clearly not the knack of it, and I'm very experienced in mopping up after feminine storms."

"Oh, I'm very human," she said bitterly, allowing him to dry her face with surprisingly little vanity. "Where are we?"

"I've no idea. I just told the jarvey to drive. Shall I find out?"

He rapped on the roof, and the driver obligingly pulled up. GlenRoss jumped out and consulted with him for a moment, then opened the door again. "He says we're somewhere on the road to Chelsea," he advised her. "He also says there's an inn just ahead where the gentry are in the habit of stopping to take tea on summer outings. But he thinks it's open year round. Shall I have him take us there? You're frozen to the bone and would be able to warm up before we head back."

She nodded indifferently, and he gave the order. She said no more until they had pulled up at a well-kept inn, most of the shutters up, but smoke visible in several chimneys. GlenRoss jumped down again without asking her advice, and soon returned with the information that the landlady did not see much custom during the winter months, but she was more than willing to prepare tea for them and make a room available for Lady Drewe's use.

Drewe allowed herself to be helped out, still alarmingly subdued. She went upstairs with the clearly curious landlady, and did not reappear for more than half an hour.

When she did, she looked more herself, for she had dried and effected some repairs to her ruined gown, and removed all trace of her tears. But she was still very pale, and did not look much like the elegant and imperial beauty he was used to.

GlenRoss was in the taproom, enjoying a pint, and she said abruptly as soon as she saw him. "I must thank you. You have been . . . kind, when I had no right to expect anything but dislike from you."

"Aye, I'm a saintly man, didn't you know?" He had risen at her appearance, and now held a chair for her. "And it seems to me we are about equal, if it comes to that," he added truthfully. "I seem to recall I was far from kind the last time we met. In fact, I owe you an apology, and have been meaning to give it to you."

She waved that aside as if it no longer mattered. "You . . . must be wondering . . ."

"Nay, lass," he said more gently. "It's none of my affair."

"The whole world will know soon enough," she said bitterly. "You may as well hear it from me."

He remained silent, and after a moment she added harshly, "Everything you said about me the last time we met was true. I am vain, shallow, heartless—everything you and everyone else has been saying of me from the moment I made my come-out."

"Nay, lass, this is not in the least like you," he protested. "I fear I should do something to make you angry, or you shall be falling into a green-and-blue lethargy next."

She didn't even smile. "It is the Carlisle curse, I sometimes think. When I arrived in London, at too young an age, my brothers and father had already done their work too well. Everyone expected me to be wild to a fault, and I . . . God help me, I certainly didn't disappoint them."

She rubbed a hand before her eyes. "They also claim that no Carlisle possesses a heart, and I should know that better than anyone. I don't know. Perhaps I might have escaped, if I had tried hard enough. But how can you learn to love when you have never received any in return.''

"Now I know you are clearly mad," he countered, teasing her. "Good God, half the men in London are in love with you.''

She blenched visibly for some reason. After a moment he said ruefully, "Forgive me. I'm a clumsy brute, lass. It seems I never know when to cease my teasing. But you should not talk such nonsense, you know. You will be the better for some hot tea inside you. Mrs. Ardle, the landlady, has it ready, and it's a thoughtless fellow I am for forgetting it.''

She allowed him to pour her a cup of tea, but sipped at it only listlessly. For his part GlenRoss was growing seriously alarmed, for he had never thought to see the imperious Lady Drewe Carlisle so humbled. After a moment he said, "On second thought, tea may be the English panacea, but I think you need something stronger, lass. It's no doubt ungenteel to offer a lady strong spirits, but what you could do with is a good stiff Scots whiskey. Lacking that, brandy will have to do.''

He fetched her one himself, and made her drink it. She obeyed him docilely enough, alarming him even more, and though she shuddered at the taste of it, some color began to last to creep back into her face.

"Now, then, lass," he said again when she had finished and he had removed the glass from her listless hand. "What is it? It can't be as bad as that, surely?''

And as she had before, she cried unwillingly, her face breaking up again. "You don't know! Oh, God . . . !''

He took her hands warmly between his own, surprised that she could engender such strong pity in him. He had thought her many things, over the course of their brief acquaintance, but pitiful had never been one of them.

After a moment she made an effort to pull herself together. "Haymont is dead," she said baldly, her voice threatening to betray her once again.

He frowned, for it was not what he had expected. "Haymont? Is that the lad you were engaged to? I'm sorry, lass."

"Yes." She still spoke baldly, and he could not doubt her pain. "I have no right to mourn him. I ended our engagement, after all. Worse, it was my fault he died."

"Nay, lass," he said gently, in genuine compassion. "We all tend to blame ourselves when those we love die. I should know. But it is mere vanity, I fear."

"Vanity!" she repeated. "I begin to think my name is vanity! I didn't love him, God help me, but I didn't wish him d-dead. He was just a boy. And I caused his death, as surely as if I had shot him myself. I shall have to live with that for the rest of my life."

He was increasingly at a loss. "Was he shot? Ah . . . in a duel over you?" he asked, beginning at last to see daylight. "Nay, then, lass, it's a sad waste, but hardly your fault. Men will ever be fools over women, I regret to say. Nor do I suspect it's the last time men will come to blows over you. It is one of the handicaps of being a beautiful woman."

She laughed almost wildly. "It is not a handicap. It's a curse! You said half the men in London were in love with me. Perhaps if one man had ever been genuinely in love with me, I might even yet have been saved. But it's too late now. I've seen to that, with my temper and my vanity. Do you know why I broke my engagement to Haymont?"

"No, lass."

"Because he loved me too much! He was like an adoring puppy, always at my heels, smiling no matter what I did. In the end, I couldn't bear it. But I didn't wish this on him, poor boy." Her voice broke again, but after a moment she steadied it. "But the irony is that even he did not really love me. He was in love with a dream, not me. And it killed him."

He waited patiently, still mostly in the dark and wondering why she was telling this to him, of all people. But then he thought of her brothers and her fashionable father, and he began to understand, even as his pity for her deepened.

After a moment she managed to regain ragged control of herself again. "I'm sorry. Above all things I despise the maudlin, but it seems I am as capable of it as anyone else. I did cause Haymont's death, for he died defending my honor—my honor!—against Lavisse. And that is the biggest jest of all."

"Lavisse? The Frenchman?"

"Yes. I told you we had come to the cream of the jest. I let Lavisse kiss me to prove . . . to prove to myself that it meant nothing," she said harshly. "And it did. Only Lavisse boasted of it, as I should have known he would, and Haymont defended me, poor misguided fool. In effect he died for nothing, for I have no honor!"

"I doubt he would say so," he corrected her gently. "It seems to me you *are* being vain, lass. I'm sorry it happened, but they were both grown men. You made them neither quarrel nor decide to settle their differences in such a way."

But she was beyond hearing him. "I have been meaning for some time to escape—to escape this terrible place and what I have become. If only I had had the courage to do so, Haymont might be alive still. It is all my wicked vanity. Now I have made London too hot to hold me, and it is indeed poetic justice. I will never dare to hold up my head there again. That must be amusing to you, at least."

"Nay, lass, I am finding none of this amusing," he said truthfully. "But as for never daring to hold up your head again, that is mere nonsense. You of all people should know how quickly scandals blow over in London."

"Not this one. I have seen to that as well, for I have made too many enemies. At any rate, do you think I could go back—to their gloating and their unpleasant stares? Oh, God! That makes it seem as if that were all I cared about, when poor Haymont is dead! And it is precisely because they will be right that I can never go back."

He thought she was talking wildly, in her first shock and grief, and would soon change her tune. She seemed to realize it, and made a strong attempt to pull herself together. "And I am indeed being maudlin, am I not?" she said with a broken attempt at a smile. "And you don't wish to hear my troubles. I should not have imposed on you, especially since you were also one of my victims."

"Nay, lass, I was never one of your victims."

"No, you saw through me from the first. I think that is why I agree to that cursed wager. I meant to teach you a lesson, for you looked at me in contempt, and that was the one thing I could not abide."

"Did you mean to jilt me too, once I was at your feet?" he asked curiously.

She looked up quickly, flushing. "What does it matter? I have already paid the forfeit to Harry. You are safe from my machinations," she added a little bitterly.

"What was the forfeit? I never learned the exact terms, and I confess I'm a little curious to know my worth in your eyes," he said lightly.

She hesitated, then answered baldly, making no attempt to excuse or defend herself. "My emeralds against Harry's grays."

He whistled. "I'm flattered."

"You need not be. It was yet another instance of my damnable arrogance. In fact, you should be rejoicing, for the joke is on me. What man of decency would marry the scandalous Lady Drewe Carlisle now? I have been notoriously difficult

to please, and now no one will have me! That is indeed
. . . amusing.''

He strolled to the window to look out on the bare yard,
telling himself he was a fool to feel any pity for her. She
was indeed only reaping what she had sown, and it was none
of his affair anyway. At any rate, she was fairly humbled
now, but it was unlikely to last long.

Nor could he believe the case as bad as she thought it. If
she was right that this would do her reputation little good,
and that more cautious men would hesitate to offer for her,
that had been the case already. She had built her reputation
too efficiently not to expect to bear the results now. But
though she would undoubtedly endure some unpleasant
snubs, and her many enemies would rejoice in her discomfiture,
he could not believe it would not soon blow over. She
was too beautiful and too sought-after for the English *ton*
to bear a grudge for long.

And while she was admittedly feeling guilty now, he knew
that such guilt seldom lasted. It was even highly probable
that she was right, and she possessed no heart. Certainly
before today she had given him no indication of having one.
It would undoubtedly do her no harm to be thoroughly
chastened for once.

And yet he felt none of the triumph he might have expected
to feel at seeing her brought to her knees. She was right:
in many ways she had never stood a chance. What could be
expected of anyone coming from such a background? Nor
was it in her nature to meekly try to overcome her family's
reputation. Aye, her pride would allow her to do little else
than rub the disapproving noses in her own behavior, and
doubtless in similar circumstances he would have done the
same.

He recognized that he was indeed a fool. Not many in this
benighted country would consider Lady Drewe Carlisle a fit

object for pity, and she would doubtless find that more object-ionable than his contempt. More, he had told Ponsonby the truth that first evening. The last thing he needed was a spoilt and willful beauty on his hands. She would find their ways and their weather abominable, and set his measured way of life by the ears.

He turned back, knowing that none of that mattered, and that her humiliation had achieved what none of her pride and beauty could have. "It seems you should not have paid off your wager so quickly, lass," he said ruefully. "Will you do me the very great honor of becoming my wife?"

11

The astonishing nuptials between Lady Drewe Carlisle and the Scottish Earl of GlenRoss took place privately four days later, to the general disbelief of the Polite World.

Drewe had not been easy to convince. She had started up at GlenRoss's proposal, a touch of her old defiance in her face, and cried, "Confound you! D'you think I want your pity?"

"No more than I want yours," GlenRoss had returned calmly. "The world will tell you you are the one to be pitied if you accept my offer, and I fear they're right. I am not of your world, and it is no easy life I offer you. You would be wise to reject me out of hand."

That quieted her a little. "Then why?" she demanded. "You will not pretend you have fallen in love with me! You despise me."

"I've never said that. I've disapproved of you most of the time, I'll admit, but you are more beguiling than perhaps you know yourself, lass. There were times I've liked you very well indeed. In fact, had it not been for my awareness of that absurd wager, I might very well have fallen victim of your charms."

"Don't patronize me!" she flashed. "There can be no other reason than your pity, and we both know it."

He smiled, for it seemed she was humbled indeed if she could say that. It was perhaps a good thing it would not last.

"Very well. Then will you believe me if I say I think we might deal together surprisingly well? You've spirit and courage, and I admire both. More, if you are looking for a reason, I will admit I am perfectly aware that you come into a considerable fortune upon your marriage. Does that satisfy you?"

She was frowning, but pointed out truthfully, "You might have had a greater fortune from Miss Gaffney. And far more docility."

He sighed with mock sorrow. "Aye, she was all docility, and I confess I've a taste for such myself. Let me but murmur that a thing was so, and she would back me to the ends of the earth, be I ever so foolish; and there's no doubt that's extremely flattering to a man. Unfortunately, I've my clan to consider, and the truth is, I fear she would never do for my Frasers. We're a rough, contentious lot, with few manners. She would have run shrieking in horror from us within a sennight."

"And you don't think I will?"

His eyes began to twinkle. "I'd back you against my Frasers any day. You'll have the lot of them shaped up in no time, and sipping tea in the afternoon with their pinkies properly elevated. My only fear is that they'll all fall in love with you, and cut me right out."

She regarded him with her clear stare. "And you've no pity at all for me?" she demanded scornfully. "Do you really expect me to believe that? You don't even like me."

He heaved another sigh. "I see you've seen through me. Peter himself has nothing on me for saintliness, I admit it. The moment I set eyes on you, I knew I must rescue you from the rich, wastrel life you led. No sacrifice is too great to show you the error of your ways. Have you not heard the Scots are great proselytizers? We think it our role to save the rich English from themselves."

She almost smiled at that. "Will you never be serious?"

"Ah, and now I fear you have come closer to the mark. It is my greatest fault, and one that has earned me no little scorn in my own country. The truth is, I am forced to seek a Southern bride, for no serious Scots lass will have me."

She stared at him for a long moment, trying to read through his foolishness. She had to admit he defeated her. She suspected pity was indeed at the back of his offer, and her instinct was to reject it out of hand. But she was still overcome enough to shudder at the thought of returning to her old life as usual. And there was a certain irony in the fact that she had thought him lost to her forever, only to receive a proposal when her pride had been completely humbled.

If he did it to save her face, which seemed likely, she knew her own motives were far more mixed. But uppermost was indeed the wish to escape from London forever—and thus escape from herself as well. No one would know her in Scotland, and life there could hardly be more different than what she was used to.

And it was probably quite true that her fortune had played a considerable part in GlenRoss's offer. He had made no secret of being in need, and her pride might at least have that to cling to.

"If you don't mean it, you had best back out now!" she said warningly. "And I tell you frankly, you would be wise to do so. Everything you said of me was true. I am expensive, spoilt, and idle. I have never in my life thought of anyone's pleasure but my own, or done a useful day's work. You would be a fool to marry me!"

"Ah, but you little know me," he said in amusement. "As for being expensive and spoilt, that will not last long when you see how tight all Scots are with their pennies. You will soon be reduced to turning your dresses, and making do with last year's bonnet. And you will have little chance to be idle.

We're no' so feckless as you English and do most things for ourselves."

She took an agitated turn around the room, scarcely able to think and certainly not knowing her own mind, which was unlike her. She was more tempted than she cared to admit, but for once she was not thinking only of herself. Would he come to regret it when he recovered his senses? It seemed likely. And this time she would be messing up not only her own life but also his.

Nevertheless she at last came to a halt, and said on a note of challenge, "Very well! I accept your offer, but on two conditions. That you will let me help with what you are trying to do. I've no experience, and God knows whether I'll be of any use, but I'm tired of being merely ornamental."

"Oh, there's no fear of that." He grinned. "Once you endure a few Highland winters, you'll have no beauty left to speak of."

Half an hour ago she had doubted she would ever laugh again. Now she could not help it. "I begin to agree with the women of Scotland. Any female who takes you on is clearly mad herself."

"Oh, aye," he agreed, smiling suddenly down into her eyes in a way that was hard to resist. "I told you we're well-suited. You have made England too hot to hold you, and I'm the despair of my sisters. Excellent marriages have been founded on far less. But you said you had two conditions. What's the second?"

She hesitated only a moment, then said baldly, "That if you change your mind you will tell me. God knows I've jilted enough men in my time to deserve to have it done to me in turn. And I won't . . . won't hold it against you. In fact, I think you should. It seems we have little else in common except that we are both clearly mad."

"Then let us drink to our mad covenant. Or perhaps we

should pray we don't end by murdering each other, which I fear is all too likely," he ended ruefully, and kissed her hand.

It was too much to expect that such an unlikely marriage would be met with anything but shock and disapproval. Nor that the true reason for it would not be easily guessed.

"At last made London too hot to hold you, my pet?" Harry drawled, in his unpleasant way. "I sympathize, but really, this would seem an unnecessarily drastic solution."

Charlie tried to frown him down. "Much as I hesitate to agree with Harry, you've clearly let this Haymont affair influence you too heavily, m'dear. It was damned unfortunate, but nothing to do with you. What I mean is, don't do something you're bound to regret later."

She had dreaded telling her brothers for that very reason, and the subject was still too raw for her to wish to discuss it with anyone. "I don't wish to talk of it. I am of age, more or less in sound mind, and the marriage is to take place in three days' time. Come or not, as you choose."

"I had no idea winning my grays meant so much to you." Harry sneered. "But I must confess that on top of everything else, I'm vastly curious. How did you manage to turn the barbarian around, my pet? It is clear I underestimated you. One moment he had returned to the wilds of Scotland, without seeming to have cast a single glance in your direction. The next you're betrothed. Accept my congratulations—if it is congratulations that are in order. I confess I can't quite see you presiding over a Highland bothy, but then, I will believe you married when I see the ring on your finger. You have, you will admit, no very good record in that regard."

"Damme, I've had enough of your sneering unpleasantness," Charlie said with surprising violence. "For my part, I hope she don't go through with it."

Drewe was both surprised and touched at this unexpected championship. She had always liked Charlie better than Harry, but there had never been any particular closeness between them. "My reputation for completing betrothals is not high," she conceded wearily, "but you needn't worry. My mind is made up this time. I require neither your blessing nor your approval. I am merely informing you both of my intentions."

"But, my pet, of course you have both," Harry purred. "It was a trifle underhanded of you to sneak in under the date, when you had already paid the forfeit. But far be it from me to bear a grudge or be a stickler for such minor details. You shall have your necklace returned to you as soon as it may be . . . er . . . convenient for me to redeem it. I have no notion when that may be, of course, for it did not go far in reducing my current pecuniary embarrassments. But perhaps I'll enjoy a run of good luck at the tables, or our respected parent, in joy at having one of us off his hands at last, may be moved to bestow a generous sum upon me in settlement of some few of my debts. There is always room for hope."

She shrugged and turned away. "It doesn't matter. Pay me when you can."

"That is like to be never," he said frankly. "But I must confess that this unexpected generosity does much to resign me to so . . . er . . . unlikely a match. Better you than me, at any rate. I predict you will not last a month in such uncouth surroundings, my pet."

She knew it was only what everyone else would say, but it annoyed her nonetheless, largely because she feared it might be true. She was by and large too numb to really take in the enormity of the step she was taking, and there was too little time, for they meant to leave for the north immediately after the wedding. But now and then, as she was surrounded by trunks and silver paper and piles of expensive gowns and furs, as her disapproving maid carefully packed all her belongings, a jolt of unreality would assail her, and she could not believe that in a week she would be in Scotland with her new husband.

She was, as she had said, determined to go through with it, but it did not spare her from suffering the usual bridal jitters. The morning of her wedding found her edgy and short-tempered, so that she swore at her maid for being clumsy and snapped at her brothers.

It was to be a very quiet wedding, with only the bride's two brothers in attendance—and she would have dispensed with them if she had thought she could keep them away—and the groom supported only by his kinsman, the dour Duncan. The bride's father, at present spending Christmas with friends in the north, had graciously granted his permission for this hasty marriage of his only daughter, asking only that the bridal couple break their journey on the first night at Waylands, the principal estate of the Duke of Chatsworth, so he could meet his new son-in-law. Drewe had little desire to introduce her groom to her father's hedonistic set, but she saw no way out of it, and so had numbly concurred.

Unfortunately, all plans seemed to be threatened by the continued inclement weather, which mingled sleet with extreme cold. Charlie frankly prophesied that they were in for a blizzard, and the newly married couple would never get out of London, much less make Scotland in the next few days. He seemed inclined to see it as an omen, but GlenRoss merely laughed and assured him that to a Scotsman this was by no means considered bad weather.

The introduction of her betrothed to her two brothers had

occurred one day before the wedding. Drewe expected the worst and she was not disappointed. It could not be said that the new brothers-in-law took a liking to each other or shared a thought in common. The best that could be said was that Harry had more or less restrained his most malicious utterings, and Charlie, disapproving of the wedding, had been indifferently polite.

Drewe was merely thankful to have it over, and would have escaped the command attendance on her father if she could. She was not even certain whom she wished to protect, for to his credit, GlenRoss had come through the meeting with her brothers with his good temper unimpaired. She had feared to see him made the butt of her brothers' malicious tongues, or her father's witty but equally deadly urbanity. But it was equally true that she did not wish to be forced to consider her own actions through the eyes of her family. She might be determined on the wedding, but it could not be denied that she was unwillingly aware that in marrying a man so far beneath her socially and financially, she was committing an inexcusable misalliance.

She entered the church in a cloud of snowflakes, which clung to her hair and furs, but not even the cold was able to put any color in her cheeks. She knew a craven impulse at the last minute to turn and run; and only the thought that she had made her own bed, with her willful pride and vanity, and now must lie in it, kept her from fleeing ignominiously.

Then she looked up to see GlenRoss coming to meet her. He was smiling in the most natural way in the world, as if nothing very momentous was occurring, and took her cold hand. He did not kiss it, which would only have alarmed her more in her present state, but merely tucked it warmly in her arm, saying, "Ah, here you are. Shall we go in? You had best keep your furs on, for the church is shockingly cold, I'm afraid."

In that moment it occurred to her that he was the most generous man she knew. He could be looking forward to the coming nuptials with as little anticipation as she was, and yet not one hint of that showed in his humorous blue eyes.

It was then she knew she could not do it—if only for his sake. She clutched at his hand and said disjointedly, ''Wait! I can't—this is madness!''

He looked down at her inquiringly, but continued to smile. ''Are you beginning to have cold feet?'' he inquired sympathetically.

In the face of his calm, she felt ridiculous. ''No . . . yes! Oh, God, I don't know! I begin to think I should never have agreed to it.''

He merely waited. ''I find nothing in the least mad about it,'' he said calmly. ''But I won't force you, lass, if you've really changed your mind. I'm no' so barbaric as all that.''

She scanned his face for a long moment, wishing not for the first time that she knew what he was really thinking. She could find no trace of her own doubts or panic there, but then, she had already discovered he was an unexpectedly kind man. Although she had made him promise he would tell her if he had changed his mind, she saw now that he would never have availed himself of that permission. He was far too chivalrous for that.

And that surprised her, for she had not been used to thinking of him as chivalrous. In fact, she had thought of him only as, first, a quarry, and then as someone who had been one of the few in her life ever to best her. She doubted she had ever seen him as a human at all, with all the virtues and failings that entailed.

Nor was that thought in the least comforting. She suddenly felt profoundly inadequate, as if even so unromantic a marriage as theirs was likely to require more of her than she thought herself capable of giving. Relationships were not something she had excelled at up until now.

But then something in the steadiness of his gaze and the warmth of his hand calmed her for some reason. She sighed and said, "I'm sorry. It's not like me to behave so missishly."

He grinned and patted her hand. "I'll forgive you this one time. I'm told one is allowed to be a little nervous at one's only wedding." His grin grew. "At least I hope it will be your only wedding. I've little taste for the alternatives, I confess it."

She wondered if it was relief or panic she saw in those very blue eyes of his. And that was not a thought that Lady Drewe Carlisle had ever thought to have about her husband on her wedding day.

12

The new Lord and Lady GlenRoss left for Scotland immediately after the wedding breakfast. It had been an awkward affair, with one of the bride's brothers striking a note of somewhat inappropriate and frequently malicious jocularity and the groom supported only by his dour kinsman, who made no bones about his disapproval. In defiance Drewe drank more champagne than was good for her, and on the whole was glad for the excuse of the snow to cut short an event that no one would have called festive.

They were traveling post, which drew the first protest of the day from Charlie. "Good Lord, you shall be sick before ever you get out of London," he exclaimed unwisely to his sister. "You know how you hate traveling in closed carriages, especially badly sprung ones!"

She glared at him, hoping her new husband did not hear. She had offered the use of one of her father's coaches for the wedding journey and had had the offer politely but firmly declined. She knew that GlenRoss was none too plump in the pocket, and whatever else she intended, she did not intend her marriage to begin with him thinking her condescending or so spoilt she must have her own way in everything, regardless of the cost or consequence.

It was therefore a modest cavalcade that headed out of London, especially for one used to traveling in her father's extravagant style. Lord Wrexham invariably traveled in his own superbly sprung chaise, with his crest upon the door, his own coachman upon the box, and two footmen perched up behind to add to his consequence. He sent his own cattle forward upon the road to avoid the deficiencies of hired horses, and for journeys of any length he would be followed by one or two carriages containing his luggage, his valet, and frequently his cook. Unless he was staying in a private house, as now, where he had stayed before and been assured of his comfort, he also packed his own sheets and pillows, his shaving stand, a number of bottles of wine and brandy, a basket containing such delicacies as his favorite wafers from Gunther's, a ham and his own tea and chocolate, and a number of other items absolutely indispensable to his existence.

By comparison they set out with no more than the hired post chaise containing Lady GlenRoss and her disapproving maid, followed by a second coach containing their luggage, and with no other outriders to defend them than the postilions. GlenRoss had elected to ride his own rattail gray, accompanied by his henchman, and the only thing to mark the exalted nature of the travelers was Drewe's own obviously expensive black, being led behind, and the number and quality of her trunks.

She was beyond caring, though the coach was as badly sprung as Charlie had predicted. She was still somewhat in shock from Haymont's tragic death and her own undeniable guilt; and her hasty marriage had not added to her sense of reality. It seemed to her that she moved in a fog, and none of it seemed really to be happening. She was merely an actor in a play, moving through her part, but divorced from her lines.

She disliked being closed up for any length of time, and was an impatient and bad traveler. But luckily, thanks to the champagne, she slept for most of that first day, grateful to escape the resentful eye of her dresser, who was far from approving of so unflattering a marriage and had been persuaded to accompany her mistress into the wilds of Scotland only by the promise of a large bribe.

If it had been up to Drewe, she would gladly have escaped this meeting with her devoted father, for she knew Waylands would be full of elegant guests no doubt agog at so sudden and unlikely a marriage, and she had no desire to suffer either their congratulations or their obvious speculations. That had been GlenRoss's doing as well, for he had insisted gently, but in his oddly firm way, that he should at least meet his wife's father.

If she had examined her feelings, she would no doubt have found also that she feared GlenRoss would appear provincial in so august a company. But in truth, she soon discovered that he showed in far better light than most of the elegant guests.

They arrived late, only in time to change for dinner and go downstairs, and certainly GlenRoss's modest evening dress in no way compared with his fashionable fellow guests'. He seemed unaware of it, and equally unaware of the raised eyebrows he received, or the scarcely veiled amusement.

Drewe, knowing the fashionable world's view of Scotland, even Scots peers, was very aware of it, and it succeeded in bringing her out of her fog a little.

The company was known for its wit and sophistication, things Drewe had reveled in before and considered very much a part of her world. But now it began to seem to her shallow and frequently unkind. A number of dry shafts were aimed at GlenRoss, which he declined to pick up, and during the interminable dinner, one of the guests, an elegant lady noted for her many infidelities, exclaimed archly, "But this is so romantic! And now you are to carry dear Drewe off to the wilds of Scotland, my lord? I confess I cannot see her there, with no balls or modistes or flirtations to break up the monotony. What *do* you do there for entertainment, pray? I've often wondered.''

He turned that aside lightly, seeming unoffended, but Drewe snapped abruptly, surprising even herself, ''My dear Clarisse, you would be in seventh heaven there. After all, the place is full of brawny Scotsmen.''

Lady Cheyney looked furious, and one of two people laughed. It occurred to Drewe that until now that sort of conversation was what she had considered normal, even amusing. But now she found it both malicious and in poor taste. She was relieved when the ladies rose to leave the gentlemen to their port.

But it seemed GlenRoss was not so placid as he appeared, for when the gentlemen at last rejoined the ladies, and the tea tray was brought in, he took her cup to her and remarked under his breath in amusement, ''Curb your sword, lass. I've no need of your protection.''

''Then you should not let them make you a butt!'' she said angrily.

''Nay, lass. I've a broad back,'' he said peaceably. ''And I'm used to it, come to that. All English think the Scots little better than barbarians—you should know that by now.''

She turned away, impatient of his tolerance and a little scornful of it. It was true that she herself had been guilty of just that prejudice, but now that she saw it from the other side, it made her extremely angry.

But she was in for another surprise. It seemed not all the great ladies there held her husband in contempt. A certain marchioness, whom Drewe knew for a fact to have been carrying on a discreet liaison with her father for years, under the nose of her sleepy husband, made an excuse later to come and sit beside her, and murmured in amusement, ''It seems I have underestimated you, my dear.''

Drewe, suspecting another barb, said dangerously, "Oh? In what way?"

"Oh, put up your sword," said Lady Rosemont, as GlenRoss had done. "I mean no slur to your new husband. In fact, I make you my compliments. I had not thought you possessed such good taste. He is clearly a man among a lot of painted popinjays. But do you think you will be able to tame him, my dear? That is always the trouble, of course. If one marries a man, one must be prepared to pay the consequences. I fear he will not play the games you are used to. And I almost think I would not like to rouse his temper, myself. I think there is indeed a bit of the barbarian about him."

That brought Drewe's eyes back to her husband, surprise and something else in her face.

She saw him perhaps as her elegant companion did, and remembered that she had first been so piqued at his contempt for the very reason that he had interested her, standing out from those around him both because of his height and because of his air of not fitting in. He even stood out in that noble company, not because of his inferior dress or lack of polish, but because he looked vital and alive instead of bored and cynical, as did the rest of the men present. He somehow seemed to carry the sun and outdoors with him, even at that hour and that season, as if he indeed would be more at home leading a swift cattle raid or striding across the heather.

It was an uncomfortable realization, for some reason, but the rest of Lady Rosemont's words fell on deaf ears. She did not believe GlenRoss possessed a temper, else he could not have taken the slurs he had received that night so placidly. And she had reason to know that he was both extremely good-natured and unexpectedly kind, for though he had retaliated in a mild way to her attack on that never-to-be-forgotten day, he had reacted more in amusement than anger. And she had never seen him lose his temper, though she had given him ample provocation.

Unfortunately an amiable temper was no recommendation in her eyes, for she usually held such paragons in contempt and thought them inexcusably weak. But it occurred to her that no one could call GlenRoss weak. He had more than held his own with her, and on at least one occasion he had decidedly emerged with the honors.

But a reminder of that long-ago day brought with it its own jolt, especially when Lady Rosemont murmured provocatively before drifting away, "You know, I almost envy you, my dear. Especially tonight."

For Drewe, still encompassed in her comfortable fog, had never until that moment considered all the consequences of her marriage. She had moved and reacted automatically, thinking of little and planning no further than her wedding day. Once or twice she had been panicked, wondering whether she would find life in the wilds of Scotland supportable, and what she was to find to occupy herself there. But she had, incredibly, never before considered the more immediate problem of the wedding night to come.

Now, with Lady Rosemont's mocking words still in her ears, Drewe saw that the rest of the company was not nearly so naive. Though the conversation continued unabated, there were a good many eyes upon them, both masculine and feminine, and no doubt all were speculating about how soon the newly wedded pair would find a reason to excuse themselves.

She could have sworn aloud at her folly for placing herself in so untenable a position, and realized why she had always found weddings so gothic. They might as well still be displaying the bloody sheets in the morning. It was disgusting.

But she was honest enough to realize that underlying her anger was the realization that she did not know herself what she wanted to happen. She was undoubtedly married to GlenRoss, and she could not forget that he had been the first one to give her a taste of passion. But he had also as plainly turned off his own passion with remarkable ease, on that memorable occasion, and made her feel more than a fool. She was not at all sure she wished to give him so much power over her again.

She excused herself in the end, ignoring the amused glances that followed her, and retired to her bedchamber, still unsure what she meant to do. Nor did it help that Jurby, her dresser, was waiting for her, plainly in much the same expectations, her mistress's most revealing night robe laid out and the bed turned back invitingly.

Drewe dismissed her as soon as possible, hating her sly glances; but she did not immediately go to bed. It was intolerable that even the servants were speculating about the night to come, and made her wonder how brides had endured it over the ages. She was tempted to lock her door and take some of her drops, so that GlenRoss should find his bride insensible of his coming and be forced to seek his own solitary bed.

But then, it was galling for her to admit she had no idea what GlenRoss expected of the marriage. Certainly he had so far made no attempt to take advantage of the situation. During the few days before their wedding he had not so much as kissed her cheek. He had been attentive at the church, and the breakfast following, and solicitous of her comfort on the drive that day, but he betrayed none of the ardor one might expect of a bridegroom on his wedding day.

That realization jerked her even further out of her comforting fog. She had cold-bloodedly set out to marry GlenRoss for her own reasons, and she had succeeded. But she had absolutely no idea why he had offered for her. And that was a new come-out indeed for the beautiful and much-sought-after Lady Drewe Carlisle. Pity there was, yes, but she could not believe any man would offer for a woman merely out of pity. Perhaps it was the money, then.

But then that was even more unsettling, especially since she was forced to acknowledge a certain acceleration of her pulse at the thought of his coming to her that night. She had not forgotten the way he had kissed her in that drafty barn, and if that was a recollection likely to make her furious all over again, she could not deny that he had shown her something about herself that she had never known before.

The problem was that although it would be very pleasurable to make him fall in love with her, she had yet to succeed in that ambition. And the idea that he should find the great Lady Drewe waiting for him like a docile little wife, nervous and shy, when he had shown her not the least sign of interest or made any move to win her, was intolerable to her.

Her mind made up, she went quickly and locked the door, feeling a little as if she had burned her bridges as she did so. She had no idea whether he would be angry or merely amused when he discovered it. And that told its own tale about the state of her marriage. She had never thought to find herself so annoyingly uncertain where a mere man was concerned, and did not much like the sensation.

Her decision made, she should no doubt have gone to bed and slept soundly. But instead she wandered the strange room, unaware of its drafts and the falling snow outside. She hardly knew whether she longed for GlenRoss to come or dreaded it. It was best for him to know at once, of course, so there would be no misunderstandings between them. In fact, even the word "husband" sounded strange and disquieting to her, as if in the last twelve hours she had somehow become something less than she had been.

But then, she supposed she had. In the eyes of the law she was a possession now, not an individual. For one of her temperament and pride, that was intolerable. She had no intention of ever becoming any man's possession.

More, it was said that every man altered once he took a wife. The most tolerant of men became suddenly jealous and tyrannical, their honor very near the surface. What they admired in a mistress or another woman they would not tolerate in their own wives, and instantly became narrow-minded and provincial.

Well, if GlenRoss thought to take her over, body and soul, he was in for a surprise. He must expect her to be pitifully grateful as well, which made things ten times worse. Theirs was a marriage of convenience, no more. And he should learn it at once.

Thus she effectively worked herself up into a temper. He was probably below, even now, boasting of his conquest. She had little illusion about men, for she had two brothers and knew what odious tricks they got up to. Nor did she deceive herself that GlenRoss would need to love her, or even be fond of her in order to perform his marital duties. He had shown her that himself, if she had needed a lesson, for he had had no difficulty whatsoever in enjoying subduing her on that infuriating occasion, even while clearly despising her.

She suddenly heard a creak in the passage, and to her fury, her heart jumped with fright. But the steps passed by, and she heard a snatch of drunken song. It was only one of the other guests going up to bed.

Gradually her heart slowed, but oddly enough she found herself torn between relief and an irrational disappointment. It was one thing to lock her door against her new husband, and quite another to have him so delinquent in demanding admittance. At the very least, it was far from flattering.

Damn GlenRoss anyway! Whatever the circumstances of their marriage, he should find that Lady Drewe Carlisle was no ripe plum to fall into his careless hands. And even without Lady Rosemont's words, she had a horrible suspicion that giving in to the barbarous Scot now would be to court disaster from the very beginning.

With sudden determination she jumped into bed and blew out her candles. She had had little enough sleep the night before, and for once she should not even need her drops to fall into a deep sleep. If her husband cared to rouse the household and make a fool of himself, he could do so, but he would find no entrance tonight into his wife's bedchamber.

But despite the comfort of the bed, the cheery warmth of the fire in the darkness, and the warming pan that had been passed between the sheets, she lay in a rigid heap, unable to relax or court sleep. Every sound in the corridor, or creak of the old house, or breaking up of a log in the fireplace made her jump. What was keeping him so long? Surely the rest of the household had gone to bed by now? Hell and the devil confound him for humiliating her so. It did no good to lock her door against him if he did not even trouble to seek admittance.

She did not know when she finally tumbled into an unrestful sleep. But she woke, cramped and frozen, to discover that the fire had died down and the dim light of dawn was lifting the darkness.

For a moment she was disoriented and didn't know where she was. Then, as she realized, she sat up with a jerk, despite the creeping cold.

He had not come. If he had tried her door at all, she had not heard it, and he had not stayed to contest his exclusion. He had simply not cared. The great Lady Drewe Carlisle had been left quite alone on her wedding night, while her husband slept elsewhere, or, for all she knew, spent the hours with someone else.

She told herself she should be glad, for it had saved her

an unpleasant scene. But gladness was somehow not the emotion uppermost in her breast. In a sudden fit of fury she grabbed up the candlestick on the table beside her bed and threw it with all her strength across the room.

13

Lord GlenRoss was up betimes the next morning, and looked to be in a cheerful mood. He strolled out to assess conditions and found his henchman waiting for him.

It had snowed during the night, but it had stopped coming down now, and though the morning was cold and crisp, it seemed to carry no moisture in it. GlenRoss sniffed the air and remarked hopefully, "We should be able to get through without trouble, if it doesn't take it into its head to blow up a blizzard. Will it, do you think?"

Duncan snorted, eyeing the cheerfulness of his master with dour disfavor. "Dinna fash yoursel'. *They've* no notion of weather!"

GlenRoss grinned at him. "Even Scots weather, bad as it is, is to be preferred, eh? How did they treat you here?"

"I'm no' like to complain. There's naught but contempt belowstairs for so unequal a match, but I've yet to be moved by the dislike o' such as them. I'll be glad enough to get home again, though, I'll confess."

"We're as great snobs as they, come to that."

"Aye," Duncan grunted uncommunicatively. He eyed his master anew and demanded, "And are ye relishing your entry into one o' the great houses of England? It's in the nature of a triumph, nae doubt."

"They must certainly think so. But no doubt they improve upon acquaintance," his master conceded wryly.

"And your father-in-law?" Duncan pursued sourly. "Nae doubt he greeted ye wi' open arms? Seemingly he was too fra' wi' his great friends to dance at his daughter's wedding, but one shouldna hold that against him."

"Thank heaven for small mercies!" GlenRoss abruptly stretched, taking in a deep breath of the cold. "God, like you, I've a sudden need to be done with all civilization and out on the glens, Duncan. There at least a man can breathe."

Duncan grunted at that, as if obscurely satisfied by something. He had taken the news of his master's upcoming nuptials to the beautiful Lady Drewe Carlisle with a horror that was as unflattering to as it was contemptuous of the London beauty. To do him credit, he had disapproved even of a possible match between his chief and the docile Miss Gaffney, for he had no opinion at all of London females. He thought them weak, spoilt flibbertigibbets, with not a care in their empty heads but their own pleasure. More to the point, none of them were likely to be willing or able to adapt to the very different world of the Highlands.

As for his opinions of Lady Drewe, they were not anywhere near so charitable. She had apparently found London too confining for her scandalous antics, and now thought to escape by taking advantage of one notoriously soft in the head where ladies in distress were concerned. Duncan foresaw nothing but disaster from such an unlikely union.

Luckily he did not believe his chief to be seriously in love with the impetuous beauty, or he would have been even more worried than he was. He knew GlenRoss had ever a soft corner for a damsel in distress, and though generally hard-headed enough, and a canny judge of men, was invariably an easy mark for any tale of woe. He had come to great responsibility at an early age, and took those responsibilities seriously, and as Duncan knew well, supported any number of ne-er-do-wells, unfortunate widows, and indigent orphans.

Not that Lady Drewe fell into any of those categories. More, Duncan had every fear she would cut up all their peace with her spoilt demands and Southern contempt for anything Scots, and end by running back to London with her tail between her legs.

That was, of course, the most that could be hoped for now, and Duncan did devoutly hope for it. But he had to acknowledge that Lady Drewe was beautiful enough and tempestuous enough to give him considerable unease. He knew his chief's chivalrous nature well enough to suspect he would be the one to be hurt, and not the heartless beauty, and so cursed the day they had ever set foot in godless London.

Duncan had, with his usual bluntness, done his best to talk GlenRoss out of so mad a step. He had not succeeded, but he was not one to give up so tamely, and added darkly now, "And if we are like fish out o' water here, what will *she* be there? It's mad ye are, and so I've told ye. Or bewitched. She's a bonny enough lass, despite her tantrums, but she's soft as butter. She'll no' last a month at home."

"Then you've no need to worry," GlenRoss said calmly. "But she may surprise us both."

Duncan pricked up his ears at that betraying slip. "Is that wha' ye expect, lad?" he demanded incredulously. "Then why in God's name did ye wed her?"

"But you know why," GlenRoss murmured provocatively. "I have clearly fallen a victim to her fascinating charms."

Duncan regarded him with disfavor. "Take care ye don't! Aye, and take care this is nobbut some clever plan of her own, for you needn't try to pull the wool over my eyes she didna mean to have ye from the first."

GlenRoss gave a shout of laughter. "I fear you value my

worth far more than she does, Duncan. She meant to bring me to my knees, certainly. But that is not the same thing at all. Believe me, she had no thought of marriage.''

Duncan was by no means so sure, for he did indeed value his chief's charms higher than GlenRoss did himself, and in his estimation the chief was worth a dozen of any spoilt beauty. ''If it comes to that, I'm far from trusting this sudden conversion of hers,'' he said bluntly. ''She's had a slap to her pride, clearly, and it's shaken her. But she's far too headstrong and spoilt to last long in this mood, if that's wha' ye're counting on. Ye're a fool if ye don't know that.''

''Yes, I think you're right,'' GlenRoss astonished him by agreeing calmly. ''But there is more to her than you are willing to grant her. She has courage and spirit, and I hope you don't mean to tell me both aren't highly prized in Scotland. And she has a brain when she troubles to use it. She may surprise us both,'' he repeated.

''And ponies may fly! She's a heartless whiskey-frisky care-for-naught,'' Duncan said, not mincing matters. ''She'll no' last the winter at GlenRoss, and she'll make ye the laughingstock o' the lads, for no man who canna hold his wife deserves their respect. And that's not to mention setting them all against each other, for it's a foregone conclusion they'll all fall in love with her. Oh, aye, I look forward to a pleasant winter indeed!'' he concluded bitterly.

GlenRoss laughed, but startled his henchman very much by saying innocently, ''Oh, but I'm not taking her to GlenRoss. Did you think it? We are going to Lochabar.''

Duncan stared at him as if he had taken leave of his senses. ''Lochabar? If she'd no' last a month at GlenRoss, she'll no' last a week in that drafty, barren place. Even yer sisters refuse to set foot in it.''

''You mistake. I'll have you know it is a castle of great antiquity and considerable historical interest, and my sisters, though complaining of its many inconveniences, have a proper regard for its place in our history," pointed out his lordship, tongue very definitely in cheek. "I myself have always had a partiality to it."

"Aye, in the summer, when the loch is no' frozen and the gales don't come sweeping down from the Highlands," grunted Duncan. "And ye're no' a woman. Wha' devilry are ye brewing now, lad? Out wi' it."

"No devilry. I am merely taking my bride to the seat of the Fraser fortunes. What could be more respectable or proper?"

Duncan, who knew his chief, said resignedly, "I should ha' known ye're no' the man to be taken in by a woman's wiles. Despite all yer fine words, ye're clearly regretting so mad a marriage already and think to drive her awa' wi' such treatment. Well, I'm no' saying it won't work. I'm no' even against it, for ye were mad to think to import such a spoilt beauty into Scotland. But that being the case, ye should no' ha' married her in the first place, and so I told ye."

GlenRoss shrugged, in no whit annoyed by this blunt speech. "You're probably right. But having done so, I have an ambition to discover the truth of my marriage before it's too late, for either of us. If you're right, and she's too soft to endure our life, I'd rather learn it sooner rather than later."

Duncan regarded him dourly, though he was secretly much reassured. "And if she falls short o' your expectations?" he grunted.

"Why, then, divorce is not so impossible as it once was. Or annulment. Like you, I doubt she will find our way of life to her liking. But she needed an escape, and I've provided it for her. If she's the heart and courage I think she has, she will find herself as well. But if not, I've no wish to keep her against her will."

"Her! She clearly possesses no heart!" Duncan said

contemptuously. "She's courage enough, I grant ye—of the easy kind that can take a fence or a toss wi'out complainin'. But that's no' what it takes to make the best of adversity or adapt hersel' to anyone else's wishes but her own! She's a spoilt, selfish beauty, and so you will find before ye're very much older, if ye don't know it already. But as for this test ye think to set her, it's as mad as ye are! Nor I never knew ye to be of so romantic a turn of mind. If ye ask me, it's fit only to be found between the pages of some trashy novel," he ended, not mincing matters.

GlenRoss shrugged. "Perhaps. We shall soon see. But as for having no heart, you've now seen her father and brothers. How much heart do you think you'd possess if you came from such a background?"

"I should have known it was only pity ye felt for her," Duncan said in disgust. "Ye were ever a great lout when it came to a sad tale from a taking wench. There was never any doing anything wi' ye."

GlenRoss grinned. "What? Feel pity for the great Lady Drewe Carlisle? She would not thank you for that notion, I promise you, Duncan."

He added, his grin growing, "As for my plan being mad, or fit only to grace the pages of a book, perhaps you're right. Have you brushed up on your Shakespeare lately, Duncan?"

"Shakespeare?" Duncan repeated in the greatest contempt. "Wha' has that to say to anything?"

"A great deal. If you had, you'd know that one of Shakespeare's heroes once set out to tame just such a bride," GlenRoss murmured in amusement. "I intend to take my cue from him. I doubt his Kate was any more of a shrew than my Drewe, if it comes to that."

"So ye think to drive her awa' by taking her to the worst of yer homes?" Duncan demanded bluntly. "Do ye mean to starve her as well?"

"I doubt it will be necessary. And I'm not driving her away. But I have no intention of wrapping up my way of life in clean linen for her. She shall learn what it means to be a Highland wife from the beginning."

He hesitated, then added as if unwillingly, "If you must have the truth, I'll agree that I believe this attack of conscience will last no more than you do. More, she's a shrewish temper, and is like to make a spirited attempt to unseat me. She won't succeed, but she doesn't know that yet. And it's at least to her credit that she despises anyone she can ride roughshod over—which seems to be just about everyone."

"I foresee joyous days ahead," Duncan said dryly.

GlenRoss grinned again. "Oh, aye. But unlike you, I am merely amused by her temper, and I think she may have more to offer than even she herself guesses. And I don't mean just her beautiful face. You are also right that I am taking her to a way of life that is very different from her own. Certainly she is spoilt and has been little used to considering anyone's wishes but her own. That is not particularly her fault, but unless she is prepared to change and adapt herself, as you say, I've no use for her. What is even more important, she will obviously have no use for me and soon come to bitterly regret our marriage. In my mind, the sooner we both find out the truth, the better."

He hesitated, then looked up and added with unlooked-for grimness, "You say I married her out of pity. That is partly true, but you might as easily say I took advantage of her temporary weakness. You may be sure her countrymen will do so, and I doubt she herself has any notion of what she is letting herself in for. In truth, I confess I have very little more hope for the marriage than you do, and I was undoubtedly mad to enter into it. But having done so, I've an ambition to discover whether I'm mistaken in her or not."

Then he grinned again, unwillingly. "And a winter spent at Lochabar should test anyone, as you say. We'll soon have our answer."

14

Drewe took care to be seen to be in good spirits the next morning. She was determined not to betray her deep humiliation at her husband's defection of the night before, either to him or the rest of the assembled company.

For his part, GlenRoss greeted her at the breakfast table with no discernible trace of self-consciousness, and if he had tried the handle of her door the night before and found it locked against him, no resentment. He assured her Duncan prophesied that despite the weather they might resume their journey, for it looked like the snow was breaking up, and they would set out whenever she was ready.

She returned a polite answer, thinking that such excessive politeness on both sides would scarce convince anyone to believe theirs was a normal honeymoon. But to her relief, few of that fashionable company were early risers, so she was at least spared the ordeal of running the gamut of their amusement or speculation at the breakfast table.

She merely picked at her own plate, but her husband made an excellent meal, working his way steadily through rare roast beef washed down with ale, and several cups of coffee. Drewe could only think that he was one of those annoying people who were cheerful over the breakfast cups, and could have gladly strangled him.

Lord Wrexham, himself no early riser, had bestirred himself to see the bridal couple off. But they were unable to make as early a start as GlenRoss had wanted, for to Drewe's intense annoyance her father insisted upon carrying her husband off for a private chat after breakfast.

She thought such conventions foolish, even under ordinary circumstances. Under the present ones they were ridiculous, and more than a little belated. She knew the legal ends had been tied up, for she herself had seen to them, signing over control of a sizable portion of the considerable fortune that became hers upon the day of her marriage to her husband for his sole use. It had been against the advice of her father's capable and more than slightly scandalized attorney, but she had merely shrugged her shoulders impatiently and had her way.

She cooled her heels for some twenty minutes during this session, and forgetting her earlier grudge for the moment, demanded of GlenRoss as soon as he reappeared what the devil they had talked about.

He grinned at her tone, but said merely, "Why, nothing. He naturally wished to assure himself that I was not likely to beat you or run through your fortune and leave you destitute. I suppose, under the circumstances, he showed considerable restraint in waiting until after the wedding."

Drewe, who knew her father possessed few paternal instincts, said furiously, "And it occurred to neither of you, I suppose, that it is my fortune. If I choose to give it to a home for paupers, what is it to him?"

"Nay, lass," he said, for once oddly gentle. "He's in the right of it. He knows nothing of me, after all. In truth, I'd have liked him better if he had inquired before rather than after the fact."

She could make nothing of that, and they set off soon after, father and daughter parting from each other without a visible pang.

True to Duncan's prediction, the snow held off and the

roads, though covered, were still passable. Lady Drewe, wrapped in fur rugs and with her feet on a hot brick against the cold, had no champagne this day to lull her into drowsiness, or anything to rescue her from her unpleasant thoughts. If GlenRoss had been right that she had given little thought to the enormity of the step she was taking and the life that awaited her in Scotland, she was doing so now.

In fact, in the cold hours of the morning before, lying alone in the huge bed, she had been forced to face both her own folly and the hollowness of her marriage. If she had ever doubted that GlenRoss had offered for her merely out of pity, that illusion had been shattered when he had not come to her last night. And to one of her pride, it came near to being a fatal blow.

Her first instinct that morning had been to refuse to go with him, putting an end to what was no more than a mockery anyway. But only a few moments' consideration was enough to make her abandon that plan. She had not much cultivated the habit of self-examination, but it occurred to her unpleasantly that not only would that indeed make her a public laughingstock, and provide the gossips with a wealth of fodder for months to come, but also it seemed suddenly to her that for one who prided herself on her courage, she had a habit of solving her problems by running away. She had jilted two fiancés, one of them with tragic results, and even her present predicament could only be laid to her craven desire to escape the consequences of her own actions.

And besides, where was she to run to? Her own father had sent her off on the arm of a complete stranger without a qualm, her brothers cared very little more for her, and she had made herself an outcast in London. No, it seemed she had effectively burnt her bridges behind her, and pride or no pride, she had no choice but to go on. If anything had been needed to finally pull her out of the cloud caused by

Haymont's death, it was that. For perhaps the first time she looked at herself coldly and critically, and did not much like what she saw.

Consequently, for once she scarcely noticed the discomforts of the journey. Jurby, in her corner, sniffed and did not bother to conceal her own distaste for her mistress's decline in consequence, but Drewe endured both the cold and the uncomfortable swaying of the coach without a word.

She had developed a headache, however, by the time they at last halted for the night at a comfortable posting house. She picked at her dinner and soon made an excuse to retire to bed, and this time did not scruple to dose herself with her drops. She had no wish for another night of self-examination.

Once more GlenRoss did not come near her door.

To her supreme annoyance, she overslept the next morning, and awoke with her headache scarcely improved. She went down to breakfast looking heavy-eyed, and apologized shortly for having kept him waiting. But GlenRoss, surely the most accommodating of traveling companions, made no comment other than to frown a little when she once again refused her breakfast with every indication of loathing.

The second day passed almost exactly as the first, with the exception that the inn that night was not so comfortable, and Drewe become aware of all the discomforts of the journey. The hired coach rocked and swayed unbearably, the various teams of job horses were all either sluggards or bone-setters, and to her headache had been added all the ill effects of a queasy stomach. She had never traveled post in her life, and was experiencing firsthand the uncomfortable effects of her new and lowered manner of living.

She arose the next morning and could scarcely face the thought of even another day cooped up in a vehicle she had come actively to hate. She did not bother to go down to breakfast at all that morning, and emerged from the inn into the cold sunlight only at the last moment. She did not think she could make any more polite conversation to her new lord and master.

To her surprise, she found that her black was being led forward, her saddle upon its back.

She frowned in astonishment, but GlenRoss said quietly from beside her, "I thought you would prefer to ride today. You look as if you could use fresh air and exercise."

It was the truth, but not even she would have dared suggest such a thing. She had little regard for convention, but no lady of her class traveled by horseback. In the first place, it was considered unseemly and immodest, for it exposed one to the stares of every vulgar person upon the road. And in the second, to arrive at one's destination filthy and saddle-weary was scarcely considered genteel.

As if aware of her thoughts, he said with a faint hint of challenge, "Or do you prefer to be rocked and swayed abominably in that tub? It is no wonder you have the headache."

She was unused to such solicitude, and said rather shortly, "I do not have the headache! And I would as lief never be obliged to enter it again. But no English lady of quality would be seen riding upon a public road!"

"I'd no notion you paid any attenti at all to such nonsense," he countered in amusement. "At any rate, we are in Scotland now. And Scottish women are not so tame, lass, I promise you."

She looked around her in astonishment, for she had not realized they had crossed into Scotland yet. Even the land-lord and servants at the posting house the night before had seemed English rather than Scottish. But then, she scarcely knew what she expected: instant poverty and tartans on every back.

But she was stung by his insinuation. "I had no notion

Scotswomen were so indifferent to both comfort and propriety."

"Oh, as to comfort, they regard it well enough, I'll concede. But as to the second, they do not consider it to be improper to follow their menfolk on horseback or even on foot. Some few intrepid dames have even been known to lead the way into battle when their men were unable to. They're no' so fragile as the English, it would seem, who melt at a little rain."

No other answer was possible in the face of such a challenge. She lifted her chin and snapped, "Give me fifteen minutes!"

"You have ten," he said with a grin. "We are behind schedule already. Not even a Scotswoman would relish spending a night in the open in such weather unless she had to."

Very much on her mettle, Drewe emerged in her distinctive scarlet habit in just under the allotted time, ignoring her maid's scandalized protests. She had feared that any husband would become instantly possessive and staid, but it appeared GlenRoss was an exception. And she could not deny that even the thought of being spared a day in that rocking coach was too tempting to forgo.

He gave her a leg up into the saddle, but remarked ruefully, "I must confess I had forgotten that habit. You will undoubtedly draw the stares of the vulgar, for we're by no means accustomed to so much style and beauty. But then, you're used to attracting attention wherever you go."

It seemed he was not so reformed as she had thought him. She wheeled her black in annoyance and led the way out of the yard.

Certainly she attracted a good deal of attention, but whether that was because she was traveling on horseback or because of her daring habit, she had no idea. Nor did she much care.

If nothing else, GlenRoss should learn that she was no less hardy or intrepid than a mere Scotswoman.

They rode for some while in silence, and it occurred to her that for all his maddening faults, GlenRoss could be a peaceful companion. Nor was it something she was much used to in her life. He did not annoy her by worrying that she was cold, or making the mistake of taking her bridle when they flushed a small animal and her horse shied briefly, as any of her other escorts would have done.

At last she demanded abruptly, ''Do women in Scotland really make a habit of traveling on horseback, or were you gammoning me?''

''Not if they can help it,'' he acknowledged with a grin. ''But you were looking to be in a megrim, and you must admit this is far preferable to being cooped up in a coach. Especially on Scots roads, which I'm afraid are much inferior to the ones you're used to.''

She eyed him curiously. ''Are you always so unconventional?''

''Unlike you, I can usually scarce be bothered to shock the credulous. But I will admit I've a love of having my own way. And besides, we've scarce had a moment alone since the wedding. Nor will we, once we reach home, if I know my Frasers.''

''I hadn't realized you'd desired a moment alone with me,'' she drawled, then could have bitten off her tongue at the revealing statement. ''But it occurs to me I know scarcely anything of your home or your life. How many Frasers, as you call them, are there?''

''Aye, I wondered when they would strike you,'' he said in amusement. ''As to my Frasers, there are several hundred, give or take an odd dozen. I've seldom bothered to count.''

''Several *hundred*!''

''Aye. But keep in mind I told you far too many have

already fled to the cities or even to America in search of
regular wages—which is still fewer than many clans can
claim. As for numbers, it used to be far greater, of course.
In my grandfather's day he could marshal a thousand swords
in a day's riding.''

"But . . . several hundred? And they're all related to you?"

"I can see you're an ignorant Sassenach and have little
understanding of the clans," he said mockingly. "They all
call themselves Frasers, but what the precise relationship
might be among us, we'd be hard put to explain by this time.
It's a system few outsiders can understand—or care to, come
to that. But it has worked in the Highlands for centuries, and
it would be a shame to see it lost."

"But you said some have already gone to find better
wages?" she asked curiously.

"I didn't say better wages. I said wages, period," he
corrected with a grin. "They get none from me. That is one
of the things I'm hoping to change."

"You pay them *nothing*?"

"Not in Scots or even English pounds. It's a complicated
barter system. They owe allegiance to me, as their chief,
and in turn I owe protection to them. If they are in need,
they have claim to my last sovereign, and they know it. But
the reverse is also true. I told you it's a complicated arrangement."

She was fascinated despite herself. "And several hundred
Frasers, as you call them, can lay claim against your last
sovereign if they wish to? It sounds highly dangerous,
especially given the nature of London servants."

"Ah, but that's where you and most Englishmen make
their mistake. They are not servants. They are as independent
and proud as I am, and would scorn to be thought servants.
The lowliest scullery maid and potboy speak their mind to
me if they think I've made a mistake, and have, on many

an occasion. In return they offer me fierce loyalty, and even their lives if need be. And the favor is returned. I can command their service and their swords, and they can command my protection and support. It may sound medieval to you, but it has worked for us for a good many years. I hate to see any of my people turn instead to the lure of impersonal gold. I fear they are in for considerable disillusionment."

It did indeed sound medieval to her, but she merely said, "And how many *are* related to you in ways you can describe? How many live with you, for instance?"

"Well, I presume you mean to discount those you would call servants about the house? There are my sisters and their families, when they care to come, for my home is always theirs, of course. That would be ten or so. And then my brother, Robbie, though I think I told you he's in France at the moment. Then young Sim, who's the son of my eldest brother. He makes his home with me most of the time, though he's in Edinburgh at the present time at school. Then Maggie, a sort of cousin who comes frequently to stay. And Duncan, of course. And a round several dozen or so of lively young lads who are of good birth and have come to serve and learn from me, more or less. To be frank, I seldom bother to count them all. But no more than fifty."

"Fifty?" she repeated hollowly. "Good God!" It seemed she indeed knew nothing about the life she had let herself in for. Unfortunately, it was far too late to ask.

15

It seemed to Drewe a mad way of life. Her father employed some hundred servants and tenants in his various residences, but they could be dismissed at will, and had no claim upon his purse. It was doubtful that he would recognize all of them on sight.

Nor had she counted on having to deal with so many new relations all at once. But after a moment she merely remarked, "If you support all these people, it is no wonder you are under the hatches!"

"Oh, Scotsmen—especially Highlanders—wouldn't know what to do with a fortune," he answered cheerfully. "And it's a good thing, since we've seldom been able to scrape one together."

"I wonder why."

He laughed. "Does it seem mad to you? I daresay it does. But to me it is very much the way things have always been. And you needn't worry. Aside from my sisters—who will undoubtedly all descend upon us once they realize I've married at last—you will have most to do with my brother. I should perhaps have mentioned to you when I offered for you that I have the responsibility of raising him."

She thought he should indeed have done so. The prospect of having to stand in some part as mother to a young boy terrified her. "Where are his parents?"

For a brief moment his usually pleasant face tightened slightly, and a shadow seemed to cross it. But it lasted only a moment. "They're both dead."

He seemed not to wish to talk about it, so she said no more. "It seems I am abysmally ignorant about the life I am going to."

"Well, we've little more knowledge of the English, come to that."

"And will they all resent me?" she demanded bluntly.

He grinned. "We're no' so barbaric as all that. The lads will all fall in love with you, no doubt—I only hope I may not have a riot on my hands. And my sisters will receive you kindly for my sake. But I won't deny that there are many with long memories who will find an English bride harsh to stomach. You're right that we are one country now, but unfortunately no piece of paper can erase centuries of bitter betrayal."

"Good God," she said faintly. "But it all happened long before I was born. Even Culloden was fifty years ago and more."

"Aye, best learn not to call it the Rebellion in these parts," he said appreciatively. "But are you genuinely wanting a lecture on Anglo-Scots relations, or are you merely passing the time? Because I warn you I'm a hard fellow to stop once I get going. Duncan would tell you I like to hear nothing better than the sound of my own voice."

"Duncan would tell me nothing," she retorted tartily. "He plainly disapproves of me. Is he one of those with a long memory?"

"Aye. He and my father were fostered together. He was at Culloden with him as a lad." At her bewildered expression his amusement grew. "I might as well be speaking a different language, mightn't I? Which goes to illustrate why the enmity has persisted so long between us. We developed in vastly different ways, and mankind is not noted for tolerating differences.''

"What does it mean, 'fostered together'?'' she asked curiously.

"They shared the same mother's milk, which puts an immense burden on both of them. You might say they were brothers.''

"But he is your servant!'' she exclaimed in astonishment.

"Better not let Duncan hear you say that. He is more of an uncle, if one must put it into ordinary words. Aye, but he serves my needs as well, and would be bitterly hurt if I were to hire a fancy valet or such. He would also lay down his life for me. I told you you can't easily define the relationships between the various members of the clan.''

After a moment she shook her head. "I begin to think I will never understand any of it.''

"Oh, it's not so difficult, once you get the hang of it.''

"And your people are going to seriously blame *me* for what went wrong between our two countries in the past?'' she demanded.

"Exactly as the English thought me no better than a yokel because I was born above the Cheviot Hills,'' he answered cheerfully. "And we've better reason for our enmity, come to that. Scotland is far poorer than England, as you will soon discover for yourself, so it was perhaps natural we'd be jealous of your country's riches. And England has ever seen us as a threat and a thorn in her side, because of our nearness. Nor have we done much to discourage that fear, I admit, for we were long at pains to be allied with England's worst enemy, France.''

"But you are talking of things that occurred hundreds of years ago.''

"Aye, but we're still living with the effects. Oh, make

no mistake, we deserve to be an English vassal, for we hadn't the sense or strength to cease our bickering among ourselves long enough to unite in a common cause. England has been blessed with a long line of capable kings, give or take the odd fool. But we've been cursed with squabbles and back-biting, and generation after generation of infant monarchs unable to control the petty squabbles. And the clans have been one of the worst offenders, I confess. We frequently hated each other far more than we ever hated the English.''

"But did you really hope to break up the union and put the Stuarts back on the throne? You have just said they served your country poorly enough when they were your kings.''

"Ah, but logic has seldom had anything to do with a Scot." He grinned. "But in our defense, we'd much to put up with from this so-called union. It was bought and paid for with British gold, and not many Scots supported it. And there was nothing equal about it. The English Parliament took the attitude that we were all little better than half-naked savages, and reacted contemptuously to any complaint. And there were many abuses in those early years. The English lost few opportunities to pound it home that we were little but a poor and backward second relation to be forced into awareness of our place."

He shrugged. "And don't forget, there were two attempts to break up the union. The first, the Fifteen, was admittedly badly managed from the first and had little hope of success. An old Scots ballad speaks of one of the so-called battles: 'A battle there was that I saw, man. And we ran, and they ran, and they ran, and we ran. And we ran and they ran away, man.' Our leaders were fools and James Edward Stuart no man to stir loyalty in anyone. He only came after the rebellion was all but lost, and added to our misery by ordering the countryside burnt against the coming enemy. He was suffering from a cold at the time, and later excused himself on that ground,'' he said wryly.

"Then why did you do it again in forty-five?'' she demanded.

"Many a Scotsman has asked himself that question, lass, in prison or in exile. Unfortunately Charles Edward Stuart possessed all the charm and ability to inspire men that his father lacked. It was said many a chief refused to meet him for fear of being seduced into the rising by that charm. Of course, he had been raised in France, and possessed much of the contempt of his homeland bred in him there. When he first dressed in Highland clothes he is said to have stated he only needed the itch to be taken for the real thing.''

He shrugged. "At any rate, he was too late. By then it had largely become a game, an exercise in reminiscence, and there was no real heart left in anyone, I fear. We played at passing our cups of claret over water when we drank the health of the king, and talked of regaining our independence. But too many years had elapsed and the English had already won.''

He fell into a brooding silence, and she stared at him curiously. He spoke of it mockingly, as if it no longer mattered, but she was beginning to wonder. "And did the Frasers take part?'' she inquired at last. "You said, I believe, that your father was there.''

He roused himself, as if he had forgotten her presence. "Aye, but he was nobbut a lad. Luckily for us, my great-grandfather was a canny old devil. He had little faith in success—we'd no better generals on our side than the last time—and he remembered the repercussions that fell on the clans then. He gave my grandfather leave to go, and he raised a troop to follow him. But technically the chief of the clan took no part. It was to save us later.

"My father went with him. He was a lad of twelve or

thirteen at the time, but he saw all the slaughter and heartache, and never forgot it. The affair on the Scots side was mismanaged from the beginning. Lord George Murray was an able soldier, but no one listened to him. By the time they got to Culloden it had already been lost. My father was there, and so was Duncan. I grew up on tales of it and the British brutality. They stood upon ground no senior officer but Charles believed could be defended, in the face of a driving sleet, and were winnowed by English guns. Within an hour of noon the battle was over. Some clans were reduced to tearing stones from the heather and hurling them in impotent fury. My father saw his own father cut down, and was wounded himself. He lay hidden and watched the English advance upon the field and bayonet the wounded before them. He was only saved by Duncan carrying him away and hiding him for weeks in the caves in the hills.''

After a moment he shrugged, as if to shake off both the memory and the unpleasantness of the subject. ''And thus ended the long brawl of Scots independence forever,'' he said flippantly.

Drewe shivered despite herself, as if only then becoming aware of the cold. She could find nothing to say, and so remained silent.

''It was then my grandfather's canniness was proved,'' he went on more lightly. ''The English reprisals were much harsher this time than they had been the last. Martial law was declared, fugitives were shot or hanged on sight, houses and cottages burned. A search was mounted for the fugitive Charles and anyone who had taken part in the late rebellion, and since it was considered that might be anyone, the English soldiers were none too careful whom they arrested or killed on sight. The ax was kept busy on Tower Hill and the rope sang at Carlisle, York, and Kennington Common. Prisoners were taken to be tried in England, lest Scots juries be too fainthearted. Nearly a thousand men, women, and children died from wounds, fever, or starvation, in jail or the abominable holds of ships waiting to be transported. Several hundred were banished and almost a thousand more sold to American plantations. My father, still a boy, was forced to hide out for months, aided only by Duncan, who was the same age and a rough surgeon at best. And I understand the atrocities they saw during that time surpassed any they had seen on the battlefield.''

Again he shrugged. ''It was then the English set about trying to systematically destroy the structure of the clans, so it could never happen again. The ancient authority of the chiefs was abolished. Clansmen were further stripped of their pride by being forbidden to carry arms under penalty of death. All Highlanders, not just those who took part in the uprising. The weaving of our traditional tartans, kilts, or plaids was banned on pain of transportation for repeated offenses. Men suspected of having taken part or even possessing some loyalty for the late rebellion were forced to swear on the holy iron of a dirk that they had no weapons in their miserable huts. The common people dipped their traditional cloth in vats of mud or dye and sewed their kilts into ludicrous breeches. Five years after Charles fled for France, kilted fugitives were still being hunted by patrols.''

''I had no idea,'' she said at last. ''It is no wonder you are bitter.''

''Oh, it's over now, as you say. I've no patience with those of us who will only look to the past, and hold on to anger and resentment. The truth is, union was inevitable. And we're far more prosperous now than we've ever been. Whether it was worth the cost in blood and pride is now a moot point.''

''Good God,'' she said bitterly. ''And it is to that you are taking me? I never doubted my own courage before today.''

* * *

As the days passed and they penetrated further and further north, she indeed began to see a change in the country they were passing. It grew less prosperous and the inns they put up at increasingly modest. When she commented on it, GlenRoss's face took on an uncustomary bleakness, and he said, "Aye, but it will grow more so the further north we get, I regret to say. It is one of the things I hope to put an end to, if I'm successful with my schemes."

She continued to ride with him each day, leaving the lumbering coaches far behind, and he was an amusing and attentive escort. He answered her many questions, rode silently when she wished to be quiet, and in every way was an excellent traveling companion. But she might have been another man—or if not quite that, a little sister that he teased and laughed at. Since Drewe had never had brothers who teased and laughed with her, it was a novel experience, and one she found herself enjoying. But there was nothing in the least loverlike in her husband's attitude toward her.

Since she was used to the adoration of her court, that could not help but pique her. More, as the days wore on, she began to realize that GlenRoss had little more expectation for the marriage than she did. He had married her out of pity, and clearly thought her spoilt and useless—a soft Sassenach to be despised. It seemed his people were not the only ones to carry prejudices against the English.

It galled her even more to acknowledge that she had given him little reason to think her otherwise. But if nothing else, he would be forced to reconsider that opinion! Indifferent inns, inferior roads, the rude stares of the populace, the disapproval of her husband's servant—all were things she was by no means accustomed to. But she would have died rather than complain, and so was forced to hold back her frequent temper.

That too was a new experience for her. GlenRoss had

remained unexpectedly impervious to her charm and beauty, curse him, but he should at least not be allowed to hold her in contempt. And so she held her tongue and unwillingly endured a journey of increasing discomfort, which gave her strong fears about her future home.

And in truth, she was by no means eager to have the journey end, for nothing she had yet heard promised her the comfortable, pampered life she was accustomed to. Used, even as a child, to servants anxious to grant her every whim, and as an adult to constant entertainment and adulation, she could not imagine what she was to find to do in the wilds of Scotland. She had been bored to tears in London! How was she to survive living a hundred miles even from Edinburgh and the nearest shops and theaters, inferior though they might be?

It was, admittedly, something she should have thought of before her marriage. And she had not even known then she would be going to a household of strangers prepared to despise her, an unknown child she was expected to raise, and an indifferent husband plainly expecting her to fail. She had indeed never doubted her own courage until now.

16

They reached Lochabar two days later, in the late afternoon, and she discovered that not even her lowered expectations had prepared her for her new home. It was admittedly an overcast and gloomy afternoon, with renewed hints of snow, which undoubtedly added to the sense of foreboding she felt at first sight. But she frankly doubted that anything could have made it look cheerful.

No one had warned her she was going, not to a genteel manor house or estate, however modest, but to a fortified castle set high on a crag, boasting towers and a keep and a drawbridge for entrance. Historically it was undoubtedly interesting, and looked to date from the twelfth or thirteenth century. But on a frozen January afternoon it looked anything but comfortable.

It was also set on the edge of a gray and gloomy loch, which undoubtedly added to its value in time of war. She was to learn that it had many times protected the Frasers from attack without or ancient enemies within, for it was impossible to approach in secret. On two fronts the loch protected it, and on the third, even more forbidding crags rose up behind, so that any enemy would have to bring an army over what looked to be an unscalable mountain to launch a surprise attack. And the road leading up to the main gate was both narrow and tortuous, offering little scope for an attack in force.

But as a home in time of peace it was indeed daunting. The bridge at least was down, offering one minor note of welcome. They clattered across it, Drewe finding that her black objected strongly to being obliged to step on a narrow plank over a frightening abyss, and was in danger of trying to unseat her. She controlled him, feeling a strong sympathy with his reluctance to enter their new home.

Once across and through the gate, she found herself in a cobbled courtyard. To her astonishment, it seemed to be full of young men who, despite the weather, were lounging about playing dice or exercising or polishing their bridles.

She pulled up short at the sight, and GlenRoss waved an airy hand. "My Frasers," he said simply.

"Good God! They look like a standing army!" she could not help exclaiming.

"No, no! Times are not that uncivilized, even here. They are serving a sort of apprenticeship with their chief, so to speak. They're all soft-spoken-enough lads. You'll find they're no bother."

"Are you saying they all *live* with you?"

He chuckled at her horrified tone. "Oh, not all of them, and not all of the time."

What else he might have said, she was never to know, for their arrival had been discovered by then. The difference that came over the men when they spotted their chief would have been amusing at another time, and certainly gave her much to think about, for you'd have thought the king had just ridden into their midst. They all stopped talking, and scrambled up, dice forgotten, cards tumbled onto the dirty cobbles, and shouting their welcome.

In the space of a moment the new arrivals were surrounded, men touching GlenRoss's booted foot, reaching for his hand, and all talking at once.

Drewe, unused to being ignored, quietly drew back, surprised and a little touched by their obvious affection and respect for their chief. GlenRoss had quickly dismounted, and did not seem to hold himself in the least high in the instep. He himself was grinning, and his men pounded him on the back, joked with him, and shouted insults, all in a broad Scots she could scarcely comprehend.

It was he who at last remembered his bride, and looked around for her. The men fell back and she rode forward, saying dryly, "It would seem that you were missed."

His grin grew. "Oh, aye! They'd no one to insult while I was gone. These are my Frasers, for my sins! Mind your manners, lads, for this is Lady GlenRoss, and she's no' used to your uncou' ways. Make your bows nicely or she'll think we are indeed savages."

They were silent, eyeing her with differing degrees of interest, astonishment, or suspicion. It was an unusual weighing-up unfamiliar to one used to English servants, but she refused to be discomposed. After a moment one of them said broadly, "Good God, man, ye dinna tell us ye'd wed a vision! What did the likes of her find to see in you, I'm wondering."

She saw that she would have to get used to such free-and-easy ways, for GlenRoss merely grinned. "The only mistake I made was in bringing her among you uncouth bunch," he countered. "It was hard enough getting her to take me at all, without you giving her the wrong impression from the outset."

There was much hooting and laughing, and GlenRoss himself came to lift her from the saddle. A more modest woman might have been highly embarrassed to find herself the cynosure of so many men's eyes, not all of them by any means approving. A normal new bride would also undoubtedly have felt resentment at being so quickly forgotten again and left to make her own way into her new home. For the men, including her bridegroom, quickly returned to their own conversation as they entered the hall.

But for once Drewe was merely amused. She had never been of a jealous disposition, and indeed preferred men's company to women's. But it seemed she was unlikely to find the adulation here she was used to at home. The men's eyes were all for their chief, not his new wife.

Duncan, who had yet to thaw in her presence, surprised her by saying glumly and unnecessarily at her elbow, "He's popular wi' the lads, as ye can see."

"So it would seem," she said in amusement, and won at least a less disapproving glare from him.

GlenRoss remembered her again then, and looked around for her with a grin. "I'm sorry. We're an uncouth lot, as I said. This is Lochabar, the founding of the Frasers' strength. You won't find it very cozy, but it has saved our fortunes many a time."

"That I can well believe," she said, looking around her resignedly. Her expectations were not disappointed. The inside was exactly what one might expect of an ancient keep built for security, not comfort, and inhabited by a number of men and few women. The floor of the great hall was unpolished, as were the tables and banisters of the huge oak staircase rising to a gallery on the second floor. This was obviously where the company lived for the most part, for every table was littered with the accoutrements of a number of untidy men. She might indeed have stepped back three hundred years in time, for the hall was also hung with banners and implements of war, and lacked only the rushes on the floor to seem authentic.

She was to discover that the rest of the castle was little better. It boasted one other room of good size, used, by the looks of it, for war councils, for it had a massive mahogany table down its center and was again decorated with all the tools of war. But the rest was littered with dozens of tiny rooms, often leading off one another, and boasting very little light. GlenRoss had said it was a communal life, and he was right, for there was obviously little provision made for privacy of any kind, and still less for comfort. Though fireplaces had been added to many of the upstairs rooms, and burned brightly, the warmth penetrated scarcely a dozen feet from the blazes. The heavy stone walls cast a damp chill over all, and Drewe suspected it was impossible to keep warm in such a place.

She thought of all her expensive silks and muslins, of very little use here, and shrugged. She had made her bed and now she must lie in it, and if she was to discover that her bed, when GlenRoss escorted her to her bedchamber, was a huge uncomfortable-looking affair of ornately carved posts that looked as if they must have been put together in place, and hung round with smothering brocade curtains, she swallowed that too. She could never bear to sleep closed in, and in fact had a horror of any dark, small place. But she suspected that there the beds were heavily curtained for a purpose.

GlenRoss seemed to see nothing amiss, and said cheerfully, "I daresay it's not what you're used to. But you will soon become accustomed to its inconveniences, and I've other houses, not so bleak. This is the best of them, admittedly, but I seldom spend the entire year here."

She was left to wonder why, if he had any other house, he would choose to spend the winter in a stone castle situated on a bleak and frozen loch, which she had already discovered had an icy wind sweeping off it in an almost unending gale. It gave her a very low opinion of his other houses.

But if she was beyond shock or dismay, her London-born dresser was not so reticent. Jurby had taken one look at the conditions she was expected to live in and flatly refused to stay, saying frankly that no civilized person could live in such a place.

It was scarcely a surprise, for she had been increasingly annoying on the journey, and had only with difficulty been persuaded to come north at all. Drewe merely said contemptuously, ''I expect to, and I had no idea your notions were so much nicer than my own. But it's not worth arguing over. I will see to your return to London immediately.''

Jurby, unused to such restraint in her mistress, immediately began to try to justify herself. ''My lady, surely you cannot mean to stay? It's . . . it's unheard-of. What sort of man is he to bring you to such a place and expect you to live here? Why, your ladyship's horses live better at home! And as for the sanitary arrangements—if you care to call them that!—it is no wonder the Scots have the reputation of being little more than savages. Nothing would prevail upon me to remain here.''

''That's enough!'' Drewe said coldly. ''I will remind you that you are speaking of my husband.''

That silenced the maid, shocked perhaps as much as anything by this unexpected defense. It shocked Drewe a little as well, for she was secretly as appalled as her maid. But she did not unsay it, and dispatched her expensive dresser back to London without a qualm. She had grown tired of her crotchets and of the exaggerated sense of consequence and had no use for a servant who thought herself better than her mistress. At any rate, she was unlikely to need a dresser there, for she could see that her chief goal would soon become merely staying warm.

It was some days before the news of her maid's defection came to GlenRoss's ears, for she saw very little of him. He had immediately been drawn into apparently unending labor, and was often gone from sunup to sundown. If she had expected him to dance attendance on his new bride, it would seem she was mistaken. But then, she was beginning to acknowledge that he seldom did what she expected.

But he expressed contrition over the loss of her maid. "I'm sorry, lass. But not much surprised, I confess," he said frankly. "It's rare you can get London servants to stay up here."

She shrugged. "My only folly was in trying. I have appropriated one of the girls from the kitchens in her stead. She seems neat and quiet enough, and far more willing if the truth be known."

She did not add that Flora, the young clanswoman she had chosen, regarded her with a reserve bordering on suspicion, and did not seem in the least aware of the singular honor that had been done her. For she was no different from the rest of the servants, who did Drewe's bidding glumly and with a show of respect, but plainly regarded her as an unwanted interloper.

She thought that GlenRoss looked at her with some amusement, but there was no time to say more. They were scarcely ever alone together, and were interrupted then.

In fact, dinner the evening of their arrival had set the pattern for those to follow. Waited upon by a disapproving Jurby, Drewe had decked herself out in one of her most expensive gowns, both in honor of the occasion and fearing to show disrespect to her new husband and his family. She might have spared herself the effort. GlenRoss complimented her on her looks, but rather spoiled it by saying he feared she would be frozen by the end of the evening; and though his Frasers eyed her obliquely, plainly impressed or appalled by her finery, depending upon their dispositions, few did more than bow respectfully to her or utter a stilted phrase or two.

She was to discover that when at home GlenRoss was in the habit of dining with whichever of his men were in residence at the moment. Drewe was far from understanding the distinction between these obviously presentable young men and what were frankly GlenRoss's dependents, and she did not try to pierce the mystery. She thought that she would never understand the clan system.

But she was to discover that these young men were both educated and obviously genteel. She did not know at whose expense they had been educated—probably at GlenRoss's, if she was beginning to understand him—or who their parents were, but they spoke English, and even French without much of an accent, as GlenRoss himself did, and possessed excellent manners.

Too good, she was to come to think, for though on the occasion of their chief's arrival they had so far forgotten themselves as to cluster around GlenRoss and ignore her, during that first dinner, at which some two dozen seemed to be in attendance, they were so stiltedly aware of her presence that the evening was a disaster.

A few made painful conversation with her, but they were obviously very much on their guard, and as obviously disapproved of their chief's marriage to a Sassenach. She was the only woman present, which added to the awkwardness, and she thought if she were to endure many evenings like that, she would soon begin to feel a pariah. She was at least honest enough to acknowledge the undoubted irony of the situation.

But then, she had been warned that GlenRoss's dependents might resent her. That seemed to have been an understatement, however. Nor could she attribute it all merely to her English birth, for it seemed more personal than that.

In fact her very breeding and beauty seemed to be held against her. It did not take her long to realize that she was expected to hold up her nose at them, and as on the first evening, whatever she did was wrong. If she dressed in her London finery, she was considered to be putting on airs. And if she dressed for warmth, she was being condescending. The mildest complaint was taken as proof of her snobbish English prejudice, and forbearance was considered no virtue. There seemed to be far too few servants to keep such a sprawling, uncomfortable pile, and evidence of neglect and disuse was everywhere. But it was plain that criticism would be taken very much amiss from her.

In fact, her worst detractors might have been excused for thinking it a fitting punishment for her many years of queening it over her less fortunate mortals. Certainly Drewe was far from used to biting back her hot temper, and completely unused to living under such primitive conditions.

But capricious and spoilt as she might be, she was by no means stupid. And for once she found she had little inclination to vent her admittedly volatile temper. If it had already occurred to her, on the journey, that her new husband was waiting for her to prove herself the spoilt beauty he so plainly thought her, it did not take her much longer to realize that the Frasers, down to the lowest scullery maid, had even lower expectations of their new mistress. To rant and rave—as she admittedly longed to do—over dinners that were ill-cooked, hot water that as often as not was cold by the time it reached her, and rooms choked with dust would merely be to play into their hands. It was a considerable set-down for one of her pride and temperament.

She had no taste for housekeeping, and had had no intention of taking over the running of GlenRoss's home. It might have been supposed that, having lacked a mother all her life, she would have concerned herself with the running of her father's various establishments as soon as she was old enough. But she had no patience for such duties, and besides, her father's houses were invariably run like clockwork by a series of highly expensive employees. Her interference would have been very much resented.

It would be resented here too, but it was quickly borne in upon her that if she were to be at all comfortable, she would have to abandon her innate prejudice. The inconvenient realities of the house she could not change, any more than the frigid wind off the loch or the damp chill in most of the rooms. But dust and lack of polish she could do something about, and though she was the last woman to boast housewifely skills and had been frequently considered by some of her critics as wholly lacking in feminine virtues of any kind, in self-preservation it seemed she would have to exert herself in a way she found as annoying as it was boring.

Nor was she much used to being tactful or considering of the feelings of others. In fact, the only thing that made her self-imposed task at all acceptable was the quick realization that if she were not to die of boredom she would have to find something to do to occupy her time. For someone used to almost constant amusements and a life that was frequently crammed from morning till night with social engagements, to be suddenly thrust into the wilds of Scotland in frozen winter, with no entertainments or even near neighbors, and only people who resented her for company, was a shock indeed.

In fact, Drewe was not much given to introspection, but there could be no doubt that her present life was completing the process of reappraisal begun by Haymont's tragic death. She was accustomed to being courted and admired, even if by no means universally, so it was a considerable blow to her pride to find herself disliked and even despised by her new dependents.

Even GlenRoss, though never showing her anything but consideration and a sort of indulgent amusement, displayed no inclination to dance attendance upon her, and was far more likely, as on the day of her arrival, to forget her existence completely.

It was indeed a descent from the heights for the Reigning Toast of London society. She did not doubt that her enemies would be highly entertained if they could see her now.

17

Those who had expected Drewe to throw up her hands in defeat and flee back to London had reckoned without her famous stubbornness, however. Disapproval had never swayed her—it had far more frequently set up her back and made her persist to ridiculous lengths in what she was doing—and she did not mean to be defeated now by a pack of ignorant Scots.

She confronted GlenRoss immediately. "If, as I understand, everyone around here is a dependent of yours in one way or another, I want more servants in the house," she said bluntly.

He raised his brows slightly, but then shrugged. "Certainly. As many as you wish. Duncan will see to it. What do you wish them to do?"

"It must be obvious. To scrub! You may not have noticed it, but the place is a pigsty."

This time she was sure of the amusement in his eyes, but he said merely, "By all means do as you want. It is your home. I tend to be too busy to notice, but I would have thought such things extremely boring to you."

"And so I would, normally," she said with some asperity, "but I find my comfort is not in the least boring to me. I would also like to make a few other changes. Communal living may suit you, but I prefer more privacy. I would like a drawing room of my own, and a smaller dining room for private dinners. I presume you do *give* private dinner parties occasionally?''

''Not often, I'm afraid. We've not many neighbors here, lass. Remember, I warned you you were likely to be bored to tears.''

She reflected bitterly on the complete lack of genial society, outside amusements, or even basic consideration for her comfort that now made up her life, and thought that a mastery of understatement. She had used to be bored in the midst of a London teeming with social events, distractions, and adulation. This was beyond so mild a term as ''boredom.'' But all she said was, ''I plan to be too busy to be bored. I have no skill at housekeeping, but I daresay I can learn.''

''Poor lass,'' he said, smiling down at her in a warmer way than he was used to show her. ''I was a brute to bring you here. But I warned you my life was scarcely what you were used to.''

She lifted her chin, reading condescension in the words and the unusual solicitude. ''Do you think it beyond my skill? I shall prove you wrong. I may be spoilt and good for very little of practical value, but I am far too selfish not to bestir myself in the interests of my own comfort. Do I have your permission to make the changes I have suggested?''

''Certainly, lass. You did not need to ask. This is your house, as I keep reminding you. Use my mother's sitting room for your own use. In fact, I apologize for not thinking of it sooner. And make any other changes you care to. See Duncan for any information or assistance you may need.''

She forbore to tell him that Duncan, far from offering her any assistance, remained gruff and uncooperative with her. If she could not find a way around him—and indeed all the servants—without complaining to GlenRoss, she did not deserve their respect. But while she had his ear she added, ''I would also like more to do. Housekeeping cannot occupy all my time, and I am used to considerable exercise. But the only time I tried to have my horse saddled to go for a gallop, one of your grooms—I presume it was a groom, though I have trouble telling your servants from mere kinsmen—insisted there were no genteel rides in the area, and refused without the chief's specific orders. If that is indeed the case, I cannot conceive what your mother or your sisters found to occupy themselves with all day.''

"Good God, I fear I am indeed a poor husband," he said rather ruefully. "But I'm afraid he was largely right. In the summer, of course, there are a number of pleasant rides you may take, but in winter the footing is mostly too treacherous to risk either your neck or the knees of that expensive black of yours.''

"But since this is winter, and not summer, and I wish to ride now, not three months from now, I must ask you to give your groom orders that my horse is to be saddled whenever I wish it. I will take the risk upon myself for both my own neck and my horse's knees.''

"Nay, lass," he said quite gently.

At first she could not believe she had heard him aright. "What did you say?"

"I said, nay, lass. You may ride out with me—and I will try to make more time to take you with me—or with one of my lads in attendance, but you'll not go out alone. Is that understood?''

"No, it is not!" she said, the light of too-long-subdued battle in her eyes. "Pray by what right do you think to interfere with anything I may wish to do?''

"The right of a husband," he said, still more gently.

That stopped her for a moment, and she colored faintly. But she was not one to take any kind of a curb-rein in good part, and so said instantly. "Then you are mistaken! You may be my husband, but I must warn you I give no one the privilege of interfering with my actions! Do you understand me?''

''Oh, I understand you.''

''Then you will give orders to your groom?''

''Nay, lass,'' he said again.

He spoke quite calmly, but there was an implacability about him that warned her he meant what he said. She was a little thrown for a moment, for though she was enraged at his high-handedness, she was not used to such quiet authority. Her brothers would have ranted at her, though they seldom troubled to interfere with her, and her admirers had long since learned that Lady Drewe Carlisle was not to be brooked, and swallowed whatever misgivings they might have felt at one of her outrageous exploits. But she had the horrible feeling that GlenRoss would be as unmoved by her temper as by her orders. In fact, he seemed totally unaware of the danger he stood in, and even still faintly amused.

She longed to take it to battle between them, for she had held her temper in check for far too long, and she had much to settle with him. That he should dare to declare to her—*her!*—what she could do, and even make no apologies for his effrontery, was beyond permission. It was time he learned whom he was dealing with.

She was not much used to being told no, and even less used to controlling her temper or considering the consequences of her actions. But some new and uncustomary prudence warned her that this was a battle she was by no means certain of winning. More infuriating even than the original quarrel was the unwelcoming realization that GlenRoss's very indifference to her was likely to defeat her. From the beginning he had proved inpenetrable simply because he saw through her manipulations and refused to play up to her tantrums. It was as effective a trick as it was enraging, and made her long more than ever to teach him a sharp lesson.

But the one time she had tried, she remembered unwillingly, she had decidedly not come out on top. His methods were as unconventional as they were unexpected, and if nothing else, had taught her that he was not the usual fool she was used to dealing with. She still did not believe him to be dangerous, for he was too good-natured for her to fear him. But she was discovering that there was more than one way to get one's way, and one which could sometimes be even more effective than a mere display of temper would have been.

It was too much to expect she would appreciate such a lesson, however. Not daring to trust herself, she turned on her heel and walked abruptly away.

It was long before her temper cooled, and she was tempted to put his order to the test right then and there by ordering her saddle to be put on her black. But she had enough experience of his so-called clansmen by then to know that their loyalty to their chief was paramount. The most she could hope for her pains was to be stared at in that impenetrable Scots way she was coming to know so well, or to be told firmly and not very politely, in accents that were scarcely intelligible to her London ear, that only the chief might order a horse to be saddled.

She could only bide her time, waiting for her opportunity. It was intolerable that he should dare to dictate to her, but he should be given a short, sharp lesson before he was very much older. In the meantime, she would at least show him that she was not the worthless society beauty that he so clearly thought her.

She thus subverted her temper in a positive fury of scouring and polishing. She did not meet with much approval from his household—but then, she had not expected to—and there was considerable grumbling and muttering. But since she also took GlenRoss at his word and immediately imported a dozen more servants into the house, they could not really complain in the face of so much more help.

Nor did Drewe make the mistake of trying to win her new Scots servants over or soothe their wounded sensibilities. She knew too much by now of the enmity that existed between their countries to expect them to accept her with anything but resentment, and so merely said bluntly that now that his lordship had married, different standards would be expected, and anyone not willing to meet those might pick up his wages and depart.

She had been afraid of some adverse reaction, but refused to be intimidated by it. But in any event, though they clearly held her in no higher liking, she was to learn that the typical Scots had a grudging respect for anyone who stuck up for himself. They would have despised her far more if they had thought her too weak to take charge of her own household.

Thus it was that instead of a constant round of balls, routs, and breakfasts, amid the flattering attention of half a dozen devoted admirers, and rides or drives in the park, interspersed with expensive shopping and other expeditions of pleasure, Drewe spent her days polishing and supervising a general cleaning of an ancient keep she would have laughed to scorn to live in a few months ago.

She had never before done such work, and while it was unlikely ever to be her chosen pastime, to her surprise she discovered she was too busy to be bored. And there was even an odd satisfaction in seeing rooms gradually begin to look better, and know it was the result of one's own labors. In fact, she realized somewhat to her astonishment that she had frequently been far more bored at some insipid party or other.

The next time she saw GlenRoss after their quarrel, he

acted as if nothing had happened, and calmly asked of her day. Her temper rose anew, but after a short struggle with herself she followed his example. Unless she chose to quarrel with him—and she had already decided to choose stronger ground before she engaged his heavy weapons—then it was foolish to snub him. It seemed there were more drawbacks to marriage than she had yet perceived, for one was obliged to meet over the breakfast cups and dinner table, at the very least, and in the day-to-day business of living, it was hard to hold a grudge.

At any rate, he disarmed her slightly by inviting her to ride out with him the next day.

Again after a short struggle with herself she accepted. It was even more foolish to cut off her own nose to spite her face, and at any rate smacked of a pettiness she scorned to show. Besides, she could not deny that the promise of escape for an afternoon, and the chance to be on horseback once more, was too tempting to dismiss.

It dawned overcast the next morning, which was nothing new, and the ground was iron hard. But Drewe put on her warmest habit and eagerly set out, unable for the moment to dwell on his many perfidies.

And if the day did not prove as entertaining as she had expected, for as he had warned her, there were few places where one could enjoy a gallop, and the ground was too treacherous underfoot for anything but caution, it was vastly more educational. She had heard GlenRoss talk of the poverty of his people, and paid lip service to believing it, but what she saw thrust any tendency toward easy indifference away from her. Some of the huts she saw, inhabited by two of three adults and up to half a dozen ragged urchins, she would not have housed an animal in. Indeed, her father's expensive racing stables were palatial by comparison, and probably cost as much as would feed all of GlenRoss's dependents for a year.

Even more touching was the way they obviously regarded him. He had said he was something like a father to them, and it was clearly true. The occupants of any rude bothy they passed rushed out to greet their chief, glowing with affection and pride. They invariably urged their hospitality upon them, and would undoubtedly have given him their last crust, if it meant starving for the next week because of it.

She might think it absurd, but she could not help but be touched by it. She herself was greeted with far more reserve, but she was used to that by now. And to see GlenRoss among his people, she had to admit, was something of a revelation to her. To see a withered crone, dressed in rags and possessing very few teeth, stand proudly at his saddle with her hand on his boot was to begin to understand the clan system after all.

It opened her eyes, and she began to pay more attention to the talk she heard. When he had first told her he wanted to import the weaving industry into the Highlands, she had scarcely cared enough even to think him mad. Now, when she saw what he meant by the poverty of his people, the thought of the poor wretches she had seen, forced to leave their homes and their identity as a part of a clan to add to the nameless flotsam in all the large cities, did indeed seem monstrous to her.

She soon heard enough to convince her of it, for it was naturally a frequent topic of conversation at the dinner table. The Highlands had always been plagued by a poor economy, and cattle reiving had been as much an economic necessity as a way of life. But it seemed that in the last thirty years more and more sheep had been imported into the glens, and they were far preferable, in practical terms, to the black cattle they replaced. For one thing, many more to the acre could be sustained, and they provided both wool and meat. For another, whereas cattle tended to be labor-intensive—and while the Highlands had plenty of cheap labor available to it, such men and their families had to be supported, and that took money—you needed no more than one shepherd in a rude hut to tend miles of sheep.

With the clan system falling apart, ably assisted by English interests, and most Highland lairds struggling for survival after the disaster at Culloden and the heavy fines that ensued, it was little wonder that chief after chief had given it up and imported sheep into his own glens. Time after time the inhabitants, who had often been on the land for untold hundreds of years, but under the clan system did not technically own it, had been removed—often forcibly if necessary. There was talk of one MacDonald who had hired an English factor to manage his lands, who in his zeal had in turn hired bullies to come in and force the people out and burn their huts behind them. Nor was he by any means alone.

To their credit, some of the lairds had tried to provide alternative employment for their dependents. One had gone so far as to envision a fishery that would employ dozens of his displaced clansmen. But whether a rural people were willing—or able—to take to a seaside existence was still secondary to the fact that when they were removed from their homes, the fishery had not been built yet, and would not be for several years. Most of them starved.

What GlenRoss was trying to do no longer seemed to her quixotic or impractical. The whole way of life might be foreign to her, but she had enough pride herself to recognize it in his clansmen, and she had no wish to see that destroyed.

In fact, she was learning a great deal about herself as well as about GlenRoss. While the changes she was achieving in his home were gradual and she did not expect him to notice, she was inordinately proud the night he sat down to his dinner, looked around the great hall, now glowing softly with polish and care, and remarked unexpectedly, "Good God! Am I blind, or have you wrought a miracle, lass? I scarcely recognize the old place."

That was an exaggeration, for she had merely caused the floors and table to be waxed and polished, and unearthed a set of Meissen china and insisted upon its being used, against the jealous objections of what passed for the housekeeper.

More changes were in store for him, for she had also lightened the diet somewhat. Even in winter a constant diet of joints and roasts with few side dishes or cakes or jellies was too heavy for her taste. She herself had seldom cared much for her food, but she noticed that though he never complained, GlenRoss often toyed with his own dinner, and while he probably would deny it, she suspected he had developed a taste for London cookery. Certainly other dishes, peculiar to the Scots and which she took care not to inquire too closely into, appeared on the table regularly, but were almost as regularly rejected by the chief.

She was tempted to import a cook from London, for she had no respect for the buxom clanswoman in charge of the kitchens. But both the expense and the fear of offending retrained her. She could not believe the woman, who was not very clean and showed neither any hand for pastry nor an inclination to learn, was an old and beloved family retainer. But with the stubborn Scots pride and peculiar institutions, it was impossible to tell.

Nor did she still have any idea how GlenRoss was placed financially. Certainly a look at his home did not lead her to believe he was very plump in the pocket. She might have paid for it out of her own purse, of course, but she was coming to learn that that would have been even more objectionable to the man who was her husband. She had never paid much attention to such things, but she was realizing that the Scots pride was fierce, even in GlenRoss's lowliest tenant. He might have married her for her money, but that was merely to further his plans for his Frasers. She suspected he would never have done it merely for his own comfort.

At any rate, it was highly doubtful she could get a French-born cook to come, which was the only one, in her experience, worth hiring. Even a London-born one would be unlikely to risk the disadvantages of such a journey and a lowering in status, and she doubted whether one trained in Edinburgh was worth the trouble of importing.

But by a fluke she had discovered that one of the young kitchen maids had once spent a year in a kitchen in France. It would seem she had spent her time well, for she had a deft hand with pastry, did not despise French sauces, and even condescended to take advice from her new mistress. Drewe had instantly promoted her to assistant cook, over the strong objections of the cook. But since she would not have minded in the least if the woman had been offended enough to quit on the spot, and the cook perhaps knew it, the tempest had blown over.

Again, if anyone had told Drewe six months ago that she would spend the better part of an afternoon soothing the sensibilities of a Scots cook—who neither showed the proper respect due to her mistress nor scrupled to speak her mind in the bluntest of terms—she would have thought him mad.

But she had her reward. The dinner set before GlenRoss that evening consisted of not only a huge joint and the usual accompanying Scots dishes, including the highly suspect haggis, but also a collop of venison in béarnaise sauce, some roast fowl stuffed with fruit, and a scallop of veal with mushroom fritters.

He had come in looking weary and strained, for he had spent the whole day in the saddle and returned barely twenty minutes before they were to sit down to dinner. But he said now, as the veal was offered to him by an adoring serving maid, "But . . . how is this? Have you imported a French chef without my knowledge? It would seem you have been extremely busy, lass."

She was more pleased for some reason than if he had paid her an extravagant compliment. But it was not in her nature to show it, and so she said merely, "No, but it turns out one of your undermaids once spent a year in a French kitchen. I have promoted her."

He said nothing further, but she was pleased to see that he ate more than he usually did, and did not look quite so strained at the end of the meal. As for his lads, they set to with a will, and she thought they eyed her with a new respect afterward, though they were far from breaking down into anything approaching natural behavior in her presence.

GlenRoss's high-handedness about her riding still rankled, of course, but she had been forced to see for herself on their outing that there was very little sport to be had there in the winter. She could not ride in her usual neck-or-nothing style, and picking her way over frozen ground appealed very little to her. But she did not much like to have the ground cut out from beneath her in that way either. It was odious in him to be so annoyingly right; and at any rate, the principle was still at issue. He should discover that he was not to give orders, arbitrary or otherwise, to her.

But in the main they lived amicably enough. She was still biding her time, and meant to hold on to her temper. She was at least wary enough of him to wish to engage on ground of her own choosing, and with some certainty of victory on her part. She was learning that much.

Then an event occurred that made her forget all her tactical plans and give full vent to the temper that had been festering so long. It was only incidental that, ironically, it won her the qualified approval of most of GlenRoss's Frasers at long last.

18

After that first outing, GlenRoss took her out with him
regularly, but it must have been obvious to the meanest of
his clan that they were not a normal newly wedded couple.
They spent almost no time alone together, and Drewe did
not doubt that most of his household knew that the chief did
not visit his wife's bedchamber at night.

It was humiliating, but she was too used to servants
knowing their masters' business to expect anything different.
But then she discovered that the servants were regularly
spying on her and reporting to GlenRoss, and she was so
angry that it was impossible for her to restrain herself.

It began innocently enough. They were sitting after dinner,
surrounded by their usual satellites, one of whom had been
prevailed upon to entertain them by playing upon the
bagpipes. Drewe had yet to accustom her ear to the screech-
ing of the bagpipe, but she was aware it was greatly revered
in her new home and played upon almost any occasion.

She was, if the truth be known, listening with only half
an ear. She was thinking instead of the tasks she meant to
set the maids for tomorrow, which made her smile inwardly
at the thought of any of her former court seeing her in so
sedate a pastime. If they could know that every evening was
spent just so tamely, and that she often retired to bed by ten,
they would have thought her taken leave of her senses.

It was then that GlenRoss used the cover of the music to

say quietly to her, "I've hesitated to speak, lass, for you will no doubt say it is none of my business, and perhaps rightly. But I feel I must at least say something."

That sounded unpleasant enough, and he was certainly looking rather grave. She was at a loss to guess what she could have done to annoy him, for it seemed to her that her life was astonishingly exemplary these days. But she said bluntly, "If you are hesitant to speak, you are probably wise to say nothing. It would seem my temper is much improved these days, but I don't promise not to take offense."

His eyes twinkled responsively, but the unusual gravity did not leave his face. "I will confess you've surprised me. I never thought to find myself with a model wife. But nevertheless I feel I must persevere. I am aware—you need hardly wonder how—that you are in the habit of taking laudanum at night to help you sleep. Believe me, I wouldn't have spoken had I not had—some experience of its addicting properties. I had an aunt once who became hopelessly addicted to it, and died a most unpleasant death. I would hate to see you follow in her footsteps, lass."

She scarcely heard the last part of this speech, she was so enraged by the first. That he had dared—*dared*—to have his people spy on her and then boast of it was inexcusable. Considering all that she had endured—and the barely veiled disrespect of all his dependents—to know that he had encouraged them to hold her in contempt by spying on her was beyond anything.

She did not stop to consider the wisdom of what she was doing. Her temper had been reined in too long, and she could not have held it under the present provocation for a fortune. "You dare—you *dare!*—to admit to me that you have had your people spying on me!" she cried, her voice shaking with her rage.

He frowned, but betrayed no proper fear of her temper,

which merely served to add fuel to the fire. "I make no apology for that, when it is something I needed to know," he said temperately.

"You make no apology! My God, when I think of what I have endured! Those same servants scarcely afford me common respect, and I see now it is no wonder! What else have they reported to you? How I tie my garters and what I say in my sleep?"

She had ever a tendency to descend rapidly from the heights when in a temper, but he merely looked amused—which infuriated her all the more. "Nay, lass, but I do know more than you perhaps think. I know, for instance, that you've a morbid dread of having your curtains drawn about your bed, however cold it may be, and that you dislike anything but coffee for breakfast. You also take your tea with lemon and not sugar, you are contemptuous of most things sweet, you like to have your own way—that at least I did not need to be told!—and you have proved a surprisingly hard worker. Nay, did you think you were not novel enough among the servants to have everything you did reported to me?"

Incredibly, he seemed unaware he was merely adding kindling to his own pyre. She was almost speechless with rage, and far past noticing that the music had stopped and they had picked up a fascinated audience. "You dare to boast of it? What right—what *right*—have you to interfere in anything I may choose to do? Did you think because I had endured it once, there was no end to how officious you could grow? Then you do not know me very well, my lord, but you soon will, I can promise you! Just who the *devil* do you think you are to dare to pass judgment on me?"

"Your husband," he answered calmly enough. "Nay, don't flash up at me. It seems to give me little enough rights, God knows, but that one I will lay claim to."

"Then you are mistaken!" she cried furiously. "I told you once before, I believe, that I give no man the right to say what I may or may not do. That includes you. Nor do I give anyone the right to disapprove of me. At any rate, do you imagine I care what you think, with your damned Scottish morality?"

It was unforgivable, but when in a temper she seldom considered the wisdom of her words. But he seemed untouched by her fury. "You didn't let me finish. I couldn't care less about the morality of what you are doing—even in my damned Scottish way. It is the practicalities I am concerned with. If you would like, I will describe to you the graphic and unflattering details of my aunt's demise, or the results I have seen in Edinburgh and Paris, where laudanum is much used to negate the effects of abysmal poverty. I don't think you would find them to your taste, nor do I think you would like to follow in any of their footsteps. You are far too beautiful to wish to end up like that."

If he had shouted at her in return, she might have vented her temper and been done with it. But his calm reason was more than she could endure. In that moment it was impossible to remember anything but the far-to-frequent number of times this man had been the cause of her humiliation. In an excess of fury she snatched up the precious Meissen plate on the table beside her and threw it at his head. He ducked and it shattered on the stone floor behind him.

His Frasers cheered.

Reminded for the first time that they had an audience, she regarded them for one impotant moment and then swept out of the room. She might long for the luxury to finish the quarrel once and for all, but she was nothing if not just, and she knew that to do so in front of his clan was to sink to conduct wholly beneath her. The knowledge did nothing to abate her fury.

* * *

She seethed impotently for the rest of that night, fully recalling every insult she had endured at his hands. Nor did it help her to know that in raking him down before his dependents she had behaved almost as inexcusably as he had.

The really annoying part was that although in the throes of anger she might say or do anything, once her anger had died down somewhat, she was prone to an unexpected and uncomfortable sense of fair play. It made her seek GlenRoss out the next morning, before he went down to breakfast, and say stiltedly, "You had no right to behave as you did, and I am still furious with you. But it was unworthy of me to take you to task before your own men, and for that I apologize."

He seemed not a whit the worse for their quarrel, but at that his face softened slightly. "Nay, lass, there's no need to do such damage to your feelings on my account. I've a broad back, and a few angry words aren't likely to slay me."

This was scarcely more satisfying, and she said still more stiffly, "My apology is not for your sake, but my own. Whatever my feelings may be, I don't take unfair advantage of an opponent. And you could scarcely retaliate as you would have liked in front of your men."

He laughed. "You wrong me, lass. Had I been seriously angry, I assure you that wouldn't have stopped me. But if it comes to that, I should have chosen a more private place for such a discussion. As for my lads, have you not been among us for all these weeks without discovering that we Scots have an admiration for anyone with spirit? They think none the less of you for ringing a peal over me, I assure you. My mother used to fair comb my father's hair with a joint stool, and she was a prime favorite among them. At any rate, I doubt it will be the last time you give me a good trimming in public."

That was, she knew, more generous than she had a right to expect, but it did nothing to put her at her ease. She was not used to such magnanimity. "You are generous, but it was not well done of me, and I admit it."

He smiled at her with a wealth of understanding in his very blue eyes and said sympathetically, "You needn't tell me that makes you more enraged than ever. There is nothing worse than having someone you are angry with behave handsomely toward you."

"Precisely! Nor is the cause of my original anger removed. To think of your encouraging your servants to spy on me makes my blood boil even now."

"Aye, I can see it does. Lucky for me there are no plates handy this morning."

When she flushed with annoyance, his grin widened, but he added more soberly, "Nay, I've no wish to fash with you this morning. And I assure you there was no intent to spy, lass. Rather, Betty was concerned for you, and rightly so. She was one of my aunt's servants, and saw what it did to her."

"Take care, sir!" she warned him. "I have apologized, but I warn you my temper is none too certain even yet. Unless you wish to have something far worse than a plate hurled at you, you would do well to leave the subject alone."

"Does that work with your brothers and your London-bred swains?" he asked in amusement. "I wouldn't have thought it, but then, I've never had much respect for the average Englishman. I know you've no wish to discuss it, but that doesn't remove the bulk of my complaint. You think laudanum harmless, I know, and no doubt it is—now. But I have seen far too many of its effects not to know it for the dangerous substance it is. My aunt, like you, I must suppose, suffered from chronic difficulty in sleeping, and she paid a heavy price for it. I would hate to see you pay the same price.

And you are not in London now, where there's a racket all night long. You should have no trouble sleeping.''

She did not trouble to tell him that the profound silence of his home disturbed her sleep far more than the London traffic had ever done, and that her sleeplessness often sprang from a far different cause. She merely said, as one goaded, ''Oh, very well, if it means that much to you! I still think you are making a mountain out of a molehill, and I will not be spied upon! But I assure you I am not addicted to laudanum, if that is what you fear. I can easily do without it. Do you want my promise?''

''Nay, your word is good enough.''

''Then you have it.''

He at least had the sense not to betray any triumph. He merely said after a moment, ''Thank you. But I must confess I am curious. Did you give it because you agree with me, or because you lack the energy to quarrel so early in the morning?''

A laugh was startled out of her. ''If you knew me better, you would know I could quarrel happily at any hour. But it is too foolish a subject to wrangle over. And I am sick to death of it by now. Pray let us leave it. You have my word, and I assure you you may trust it.''

''I never doubted it. For all your faults, I long ago noticed that you have an odd and unexpected sense of justice, lass.''

She was slightly appeased, and would have turned away then had he not reached out a hand and said lightly, but with a slightly crooked smile. ''No, stay, lass. I have been meaning to say something else to you for some time. No, don't poker up! It is not another scold. But I begin to think we might deal better together than we have done.''

She paused, his hand on her arm. She was surprised to discover she was feeling slightly breathless for some reason. ''Could we?''

"I think so. I will admit you have fitted in here better than I would have expected. You have done wonders with the place, and thrown yourself into a way of life that is foreign to you and, I know, not much to your taste." His grin grew more twisted. "If it is time for apologies, I have one to make to you. I always knew you had courage, but I confess I doubted you had the sort of staying power that is far beyond mere physical courage. You have proved me wrong."

It was indeed a handsome apology—far handsomer than hers. She hardly knew what to make of it, and was surprised to find herself suddenly almost shy. "Indeed?" she managed. "In what way?"

"In every way. I think neither of us had many expectations for our marriage. It was perhaps inevitable, for our ways of life were so different, and we hardly came to it in the usual way. But I begin to think that my reservations, at least, were unfounded. I promise you I am more . . . appreciative than you perhaps know."

"What are you trying to say?" For some reason her voice sounded slightly breathless even to her own ears.

He gave his crooked smile. "Why, merely that we might . . . deal together far better than we have. Lass—"

But she was never to know what he would have said, for they were interrupted. One of the servants came flying up then with the intelligence that my lord's sister had just that moment arrived from Edinburgh.

GlenRoss hesitated, then shrugged. "Perhaps it is just as well," he said oddly. "Come downstairs and meet my sister, lass. I think you will like her."

19

It was evident that brother and sister were close. At first sight of GlenRoss, his sister shrieked "Ian!" and launched herself into his arms.

She proved to be of middle height, dark like her brother, and with the same engaging twinkle. But whereas he was careless of dress, she was attired extremely modishly in a dark pelisse that Drewe did not hesitate to place as coming from Paris.

He received her laughingly, and kissed her soundly. Drewe, unused to such public demonstrations—or indeed such obvious affection between siblings—hung back, eyeing the touching scene with curiosity.

GlenRoss turned as she arrived, with his arm still about his sister. "Ah, this is my sister Lillibet—Lady Sinclair, I should say, except that it sometimes seems she will never grow up to be worthy of such a title. Lillibet, my wife, Drewe."

Lillibet eyed her new sister-in-law frankly. "Well, now that I see you, of course I understand!" she declared in what seemed to be her frank style. "I wondered what on earth had possessed my staid brother to bring a bride home with him, especially one of the enemy. But you are very beautiful."

"Lillibet!"

"Oh, pooh! She must be prepared for your sisters to be

vastly curious. Especially since we have been throwing dazzling beauties at your head for years.''

''And our marriage was so very sudden,'' Drewe agreed bluntly. ''You must indeed by curious.''

Lady Sinclair twinkled at her. ''Well, that too. I confess I was never more astonished than when I got his letter, for usually, you know, my annoying brother is far too busy with his schemes and responsibilities to pay attention to anything else. But if you managed to overcome his reserve and get him into anything approaching an elopement, you must be special indeed!''

''Leave off quizzing her, Lillibet. You'll have plenty of time for that later, when I'm not around to be embarrassed. Tell me instead why the devil you didn't let me know you were coming. By the looks of the trunks you brought with you, you mean to remain for at least six months.''

She laughed up at him. ''Just a few necessities, upon my word. Jeanne would have come too, but you know she is increasing at the moment, and so thought it best not to attempt the trip. And Margaret, as you know, can't get away until the end of term, though she did her best to convince Jeanne to let her come. So I am all of the family available to look over your new bride and make sure that she is acceptable.''

She went on for some time very much in that strain, for it was apparent she was of an irrepressible nature. Drewe found little in common with her, for Lady Sinclair's talk was all of her children, three daughters whom GlenRoss pronounced to be already practicing their wiles on his sex, and of the trials and tribulations of moving into a new house, only just finished by the builders.

There was certainly no more time for private conversation. Drewe didn't know whether to be glad or sorry for the interruption. Consciously or unconsciously, she had meant to bring GlenRoss to her feet from the beginning, and her marriage had not changed that. But she had found herself suddenly feeling breathless and a little frightened at words that seemed to hint that he wanted a closer understanding between them.

As on her wedding night, she seemed not to know her own mind, which was unlike her. She feared no man, certainly, but he affected her in a way no other man ever had. For perhaps the first time in her long campaign to subjugate him, launched out of pride and pique, it occurred to her that she might be the one lost, not him, were the relationship to change between them.

But if they had had little privacy before, they had even less now. At least dinners were a great deal livelier for Lillibet's presence, for she was full of the latest *on-dits* from Edinburgh, and even Paris, where it appeared she and her husband had been the summer before. "Would you believe it?" she cried. "Aberdeen offered for Barbara Leslie, and she accepted him! You must know," she added to Drewe, "that hers was one of the most determined caps set at my brother here. News of his unexpected marriage broke more than a few hearts in Edinburgh, I can tell you."

"Oh, aye, I'm a great one for the ladies," agreed GlenRoss easily. "You didna know you were so lucky to snag me, did you, lass?"

Lillibet laughed. "You should at least know by now that my brother is never serious. And I could tell of a few broken hearts, if I cared to. By the bye, Maggie is in Edinburgh and sends her love, but I hesitate to tell you, under the circumstances."

"Is hers another heart that was broken by our marriage?" inquired Drewe dryly.

"Oh, well, as to that it would be rude to say, for she is a sort of cousin of ours, and you will be bound to meet her. Which reminds me, Ian. One of your poor wretches who insisted upon going to Edinburgh looking for work was arrested for taking part in the militia riots and has been sentenced to be transported. James did what he could to help him, of course, but you know what some of the justices are.''

GlenRoss frowned. "Who was it? I haven't heard anything of this.''

"No, I think the poor fool was embarrassed to appeal to you, for you warned him how it would be. It is Angus, son of old Archie. Do you remember? I know well Archie would have tried to talk him out of it, for he was ever a proud, stubborn old fellow. He told James he found no work, as anyone could have predicted, and thus seems to have been ripe for listening to seditious talk, but I don't think he was ever really a member of the United Scotsmen. He certainly seems too broken now to ever have been a republican. I know you have a sneaking sympathy for the United Scotsmen, Ian, but I think they have a deal to answer for.''

Drewe was looking between them with curiosity. "What are you talking about? Are there riots taking place even now?''

Lillibet looked uncertain, as though she feared she had said something she shouldn't have. But GlenRoss answered in his calm way, "I told you resentment against English rule was by no means completely dead, lass. In the last few years we have had a foolish group calling themselves the United Scotsmen, who have taken the revolution in France as their model. It was all nonsense, and they would have disappeared by themselves if our government had not overreacted. But I fear this last year has been a hard one, which added to their grievances, for there have been bad harvests and high prices. Even in your own country the peasants came close to insurrection, and you know of the naval mutinies at Nore and Spithead. The king's own carriage was mobbed in London by ragged men crying out for bread. But instead of doing something about lowering prices or feeding the starving, both of our governments merely cracked down on the protestors. We passed a Militia Act last year, ostensibly to raise troops to use in defense against the French, but in reality to use against civil disorder. And in July a law was passed making the United Scotsmen all liable for transportation. It is evidently that that one of my clan has fallen foul of. Worse, young Angus is something of a half-wit. A foolish, harmless dupe.''

"What will you do?" his sister asked.

He shrugged. "I doubt if I can get his sentence vacated, but I'll see that he has money for a new start. Australia may not be a bad place for him, for he's a hard enough worker."

Drewe was observing her husband. He talked of this man as if he were his father, but she suspected that Angus could not be much younger, if any, than GlenRoss. It was indeed a strange system. Her father would not have troubled himself so over one of his dependents. She doubted he even knew them all. "Do you interest yourself this far in every one of your clansman who may get in trouble?" she asked curiously.

GlenRoss grimaced. "Yes, but in this case, I am somewhat to blame, I fear. I admittedly tried to talk him out of going to Edinburgh, seeking his fortune as he called it, but I should have found him employment there, since he was determined."

"Good God!" his sister said forcefully. "He was a grown man and knew what he was doing. And it is not as if you don't have enough to do! I am sorry for him as well, but you always take your responsibilities far too seriously!"

"Aye, but that is why I am the chief, not you," her brother said in amusement.

Drewe was still watching this meeting between brother and sister in interest. "And you have how many Frasers?" she asked even more dryly.

"Yes, indeed!" Lillibet said roundly. "Ian thinks himself personally responsible for all of them! And whatever he may have told you, I can promise you some of them are a shiftless lot, very content to leave all responsibility to him. It puts me out of all patience sometimes."

"And thus speaks a Sinclair by marriage," GlenRoss teased her.

"Oh, well, I daresay I do get carried away. But it annoys me to see you working yourself to the bone for them. And you are looking fagged to death, so don't try to tell me you aren't!" She then seemed to realize that this was scarcely a felicitous comment to make to her newly married brother, and flushed a little. "Well, I don't care! If Drewe has any sense she will drag you away for a long holiday. I think she is a saint to have put up with you this far without complaint. You can't tell me you aren't neglecting her."

GlenRoss smiled wryly. "That is exactly what we were discussing when your arrival so rudely interrupted us. I begin to think I have indeed been neglecting my bride. Well, lass, what do you say? Would you like to escape to Edinburgh for a few weeks? It is hardly London, but you would be able to shop and be entertained and dazzle Edinburgh's unsophisticated society. I fear I cannot get away just now, but my flighty sister could escort you and show you the sights."

Drewe was surprised and a little touched. But after a moment she surprised herself very much by saying, "Thank you, but I have no need to shop, and I am quite happy here."

"Good God!" exclaimed Lady Sinclair. "You must indeed be besotted with my brother to say so! I have been here something less than a day, and already I have been reminded of all of Lochabar's disastrous inconveniences—although I must say you have done wonders with it. It is looking better than I can ever remember seeing it before. But as for having no need to shop, when did a woman ever wait for that? I am sure you will find the shops all vastly inferior to those in London, but we do get more French designs than you do, and you will indeed make a stir in Edinburgh. For my part, I shall enjoy watching all the jealous biddies shrivel with envy when they catch sight of you.''

"My sister ever had a generous spirit," commented GlenRoss. "But are you sure, lass? You have had your nose to the grindstone long enough.''

Drewe had found Lillibet's comments about Lochabar somewhat puzzling, but she discovered she indeed had no real desire to remove to Edinburgh. She had been longing only to escape for weeks now, and had found herself remembering even the most tedious party in London with unexpected nostalgia, but now that reprieve was offered her, she had no real desire to take it. As for the promised shopping, she had always had whatever she wanted, and it astonished her now to realize how long it had been since she had purchased some expensive trinket for herself. Her demands used to be insatiable, and a day seldom went by that she did not discover something she could not live without. Just as frequently, she would discover once she got it home that it did not amuse her after all, and her closets and drawers had been crammed with things she had grown tired of.

But among so much poverty she discovered that she had little taste for luxuries anymore. Of what use was a new ball dress or a diamond necklace, which she had little cause to wear anyway, when its cost might feed a family of half a dozen for years?

The realization of how much she had changed in a few short weeks left her stunned. She did not know quite when it had happened, but the truth was she had begun to enjoy her new life and new responsibilities. Conditions were admit-

tedly primitive, and she saw the same faces day after day—
a fate she would once have regarded as little better than
purgatory. But she had discovered an unexpected satisfaction in seeing the fruits of her own labor transform Lochabar,
if only slightly. She had concentrated all the energy she used
to spend on her sports and causing scandals, and for the first
time set herself to a legitimate task, and it felt good to her.
If she could be magically wafted back to England tomorrow,
her marriage a figment of some nightmare, she was not sure
she would go.

That thought stunned her more than all the rest. Her biggest
failure—and she was not one accustomed to failing—was that
GlenRoss had yet to fall at her feet. Worse, he showed not
the slightest inclination to fall in love with her, nor betrayed
the least awareness of the fact he had snatched one of the
biggest prizes of the *ton* in the face of her many ardent
admirers. He had brought her to an out-of-the-way home that
boasted few of the comforts she was accustomed to, and then
added to his offense by mostly ignoring her. If anyone had
said Lady Drewe Carlisle would put up with such treatment
for as much as a day, her many admirers, and even her
detractors, would have thought him crazy.

And yet, even the annoying failure of her husband to show
her the proper adoration she was used to was no longer such
a source of annoyance to her. She discovered that if she could
turn GlenRoss into one of the mincing, painted puppies she
was used to, who danced attendance on her and gratified her
every whim, she would not do so. She had no real desire
any longer to have him at her feet, for she respected him
too much.

That was indeed a facer, and distracted her so much she
was unaware GlenRoss was waiting for an answer, or that
his sister was regarding her in growing interest. Had she,
Drewe Carlisle, fallen in love with a man who cared nothing

for her? It would undoubtedly be ironic if it were true, but she had grown so used to thinking she possessed no heart that she had not even stopped to consider it before.

But no. She was forced to admit she liked him very well, but he annoyed her and ignored her and treated her very much as he did one of his Frasers. And she did not feel in the least like one of the lovesick fools she had been used to have at her feet. She did not pine for his presence, or feel jealous of his clan, who occupied far more of his attention than she did.

And, while she had admittedly set about to bring his house to order, that had been for her own sake, not his. She might be pleased that he enjoyed his dinner more these days, and had noticed the results of her labors. But she had not done it for him, or at least not primarily. And while she was coming to admire and respect his work, and what he was trying to do to save his clain, she did not pass up a trip to Edinburgh merely because the thought of spending so much when he so obviously needed every penny he could raise was unwelcome to her. She had merely discovered that Edinburgh held no lure for her at the moment.

No, it could not be true. The thought of being in love with anyone was frightening to her, for she was a Carlisle, after all. To be in love was to give someone too much power over one, and that she had long ago sworn never to do. Besides, she was too selfish, too quick-tempered, too set in her own ways to know how to love anyone. She had never in her life considered anyone else's wishes but her own, and possessed none of the feminine virtues, such as self-sacrifice or loyalty or tenderness.

Only belatedly aware that GlenRoss had asked her a question and was waiting for an answer, she said rather abruptly, "No, I have no wish to go, thank you. Perhaps another time."

But her thoughts were in an uncharacteristic whirl, and she retired that night as early as she dared, on the pretext of leaving brother and sister together to enjoy a comfortable gossip.

On reflection, it seemed to her that without her quite knowing how, she had changed completely since coming to Scotland, so that she did not even know herself any longer. Certainly her old life seemed so alien to her that it might have happened to someone else.

The idea unnerved and vaguely frightened her. She, who never feared a fence, and had once faced without a blink a highwayman who held up her coach, felt a nameless fear, as if she were in danger of venturing onto land wholly new to her, and from which she might never return. It was true that GlenRoss had appealed to her from the first—when he wasn't making her extremely furious, that is. She had even meant to marry him if she could trick him into it—though as it turned out she had had woefully inadequate ideas about the sort of life he led. But again, it had been for her own ends, and there had been not the least sentimentality in it.

Of course she was not in love with GlenRoss. But still, she had never been in more need of her drops to help her sleep, for she tossed and turned for hours. Only stubbornness kept her from reaching for them. She had promised GlenRoss she would not, and she did not go back on her word. It was one of her few virtues, God knew.

She did not know when she at last drifted into a troubled sleep, for her dreams were as fantastic as her waking thoughts. It was one of the reasons she had begun using the drops in the first place, for since childhood she had had a recurring nightmare that despite her knowing the cause of it never grew less harrowing. As a spoilt and willful child she had once had a governess who locked her in a dark cupboard as punishment, and it was the reason she still disliked being enclosed in a small space.

But in her dream, it was as if she were in a coffin and had been buried alive. It was always the same, for she could not move her arms and legs, and though she strained her eyes open, there was no light to see and no sound but her own tortured breathing. She could feel the dirt weighing down on her, and the narrow confines of her cell, and the panic she felt was almost unbearable. There was no hope of rescue, for they had buried her knowing she was alive, and soon the air would be used up. Even her cries and the tears on her cheeks were using up precious oxygen, and she could never make up her mind in the dream whether it would be better to die quickly or keep hoping for a miracle. But she knew instinctively that there was no miracle. There had never been any miracles for her.

How long she was in the throes of the dream, she had no way of knowing. She woke to full consciousness to find GlenRoss, in his shirtsleeves, bending over her, saying sharply, "Lass, wake up! It's nobbut a bad dream. Wake up."

No one had ever come to her before. She gasped, her cheeks wet and her breath coming in labored gasps, and without thought threw herself in his arms. "Oh, God! Hold me! Don't let me go."

20

It took Drewe several moments to throw off the lingering effects of her nightmare and realize what she had done. When she did, she drew away, saying quickly and in confusion, "I'm sorry! I don't know what came over me. What are you doing here?"

She still sounded unlike herself, and he scanned her face in the light of the single candle he had carried in with him and set hurriedly on the nightstand. "Nay, lass, don't apologize. I was just going to bed when I heard you call out. It must have been quite a dream."

"Yes . . . no. It is one I have had since a child."

"Is that why you take laudanum drops?" he asked gently. "Lass, you should have told me. It would make no difference to my dislike of its long-term use, but at least I would have been more sympathetic."

She sat up a little more and hurriedly palmed away the tears left on her cheeks. She always hated being caught out in any weakness, and so said more harshly than she had intended, "I said it is nothing! As for my drops, I have given my word I will not use them, and whatever else I am capable of, I don't go back on my word."

"Aye, so I am beginning to see," he said oddly. "What is the dream? Can you talk about it?"

She had escaped it less than she had thought, for it came quickly back to her, and she shivered at the reminder. "I don't know. It is stupid," she said impatiently. "It's always the same. I am being buried alive. Not . . . not by accident, but on purpose. In a coffin. But I am not dead yet, and they know it."

"Who are 'they'?"

"I told you it's stupid. I don't know. Not a . . . specific enemy." Her voice had grown more disturbed as she was pulled back into the horror of the dream. "I can feel the dirt above me, and all around, pressing on me, but I can't move, and no one will hear my screams. I think it is that feeling of helplessness that I hate most. It is . . . horrible." She shuddered despite herself.

"I should think so. A terrifying nightmare indeed. But it is only a dream when all's said and done, lass," he said soothingly. "You say you have had it from a childhood?"

Once more she tried to shake off the mood, embarrassed to be found vulnerable. "Yes. I suspect it was because I had a nurse once who used to lock me in a cupboard when I misbehaved. But knowing the cause of it and stopping the dreams seem to be two very different things."

He was seated on the edge of her bed, and was in his shirt-sleeves, but for once the twinkle was quite missing from his blue eyes. "I begin to see why you hate having your bed curtains drawn, and dislike enclosed spaces," he said thoughtfully. "Poor lass. Was there no one to liberate you, then?"

She gave a rather harsh laugh. "You must have seen we are hardly a loving family. My mother died when I was still in leading strings, and my father was neither a grieving widower nor a doting father. My brothers were away at school, and I was left largely to the devices of a hired staff. Occasionally they were kind to me, but far more often I was merely considered a nuisance, and they regarded me as little as they thought they could get by with. The nurse who used to lock me in the closet was by no means the worst offender."

"Poor lass," he said quietly again. "Had you no one who was fond of you? You must have been a fetching little thing, even then."

"No. I was awkward and stubborn and rebellious, and far from lovely. All knees and taffee-colored hair."

He chuckled. "I would like to have seen you then."

"You would have been disappointed. I couldn't wait until I grew up. I swore at the age of ten that if I ever escaped, no one would have that kind of power over me again. And I meant it."

"So that is why you kept breaking engagements," he said in amusement. "But what of your brothers? Surely they came home on holidays and teased and spoiled their little sister?"

She shrugged a shoulder left bare by her expensive silk-and-lace night robe. "I certainly used to trail them around like a tantony pig, but they were far from doting on me. In fact, they soon broke me of my devotion in a brutal fashion. I told you once they abandoned me miles from home and left me to make my way home by myself. When I was five, Harry, who was twelve at the time, dared me to walk the high wall around our garden. He won the dare, for I tumbled off and broke my collarbone. So you see, the spoilt young woman that you so much despise was hardly indulged from the hour of her birth. I daresay you were more spoilt than I."

GlenRoss was touched despite himself. She looked very different in the dim candlelight, the tearstains still on her cheeks, her eyes wide with the lingering effects of her nightmare still in them. Her tawny hair, which she never bundled under a cap, tumbled about her white shoulders and she looked beautiful and infinitely desirable. But he knew it was not her beauty that threatened to undermine his resolve. He had been in danger of forgetting his vow to himself on only two occasions, and on both she had been very far from the imperious Lady Drewe Carlisle of her reputation.

He knew a wise man would have withdrawn at that junction. She was mostly over her dream, and he would be a fool to again allow a momentary pity to make him forget all his resolutions. Instead he found himself smoothing the tumbled hair back from her face, surprised to discover that his hand trembled a little. But then, perhaps he was not so surprised after all. "Poor lass," he said lightly.

She looked up, startled at the unexpected caress. It had never been the least part of her charm for him that she seemed to hold her own beauty amazingly cheap, for all her reputation, and could sometimes be unexpectedly shy. Her breath caught audibly, as if only then had she become aware of the intimacy of the situation, and the moment held, spun out in golden candlelight. Surprisingly, it was she who dropped her eyes first, an unaccustomed color in her pale face.

"I must . . . You should . . . I am all right now," she said with a confusion that was new to her. "You need not stay any longer."

He thought he was indeed mad, but knew philosophically that this moment had been inevitable from the first. She had surprised him with her ability to adapt and her willingness to make the most of an unpleasant situation. But no more than at her chastened mood when young Haymont died did he dare trust that the change would be more than temporary. It had not been long before she was slinging plates at his head.

In fact, if he were not careful, all his plans would be for naught. But he discovered a man could grow tired of being careful. He said doubtfully, "And will you sleep now?"

When she shuddered instinctively, he added, "I thought not. And nor will I. What shall we do to pass the time? We could play cards, I suppose," he offered humorously. "Or discuss my sister's many infuriating habits."

But his hand went again to her hair, as if against his will, and she could not mistake that cards and gossip were very far from what was in his mind.

Nor did she pretend to misunderstand. She first flushed and then paled, and said harshly, as if to break the spell between them, "Damn you, d'you think I want your pity?"

"You have never had that." But he knew it was not true. He profoundly pitied her. Of their own will, both hands cupped her face, her rich hair flowing over them, as if he could somehow give her the comfort she had lacked all her life.

It was ironic. He knew she had meant to have him at her feet from the beginning; but now that she had won, it was she who was unready. "No!" she cried sharply.

He smiled tenderly at this unprecedented panic. He had learned on a never-to-be-forgotten occasion long ago that Lady Drewe Carlisle was not always so arrogant and sure of herself.

"Nay, lass," he said deeply. "We both knew this moment was inevitable from the first."

"No!" she cried again, more harshly. "Devil take you, d'you think I am to be had at your convenience? You feel sorry for me now, but you have made no move toward me before this."

"What I think is that we have been playing at cross-purposes too long. Whatever we feel toward one another—and God knows what that is—I knew this moment would come. You have haunted me night and day. That should at least set you preening, lass, for you meant to subjugate me, didn't you?"

"No! Oh, perhaps at first!" she admitted bitterly. "But you were equally determined not to fall victim to my fatal charm. Do you think I don't know why you stayed away from me? And now it is too late."

It occurred to him there was more to her agitation than mere pique or wounded pride. He said slowly, gathering her restless hands in his and forcing them to stillness, "What is it, lass? What are you afraid of?"

"Nothing! Everything! Haven't you discovered yet that I am not like other women?" she demanded hoarsely. "I have no softer side, no feminine emotions or gentle sympathy. You were right about me from the first. Because I have taken on a few housewifely duties, and cried upon your shoulder tonight, you suddenly think I am weak and compliant. Well, the more fool you! And we will both of us come to regret this."

"Nay, lass, this does not sound like the beautiful Lady Drewe Carlisle," he said in amusement.

She laughed almost wildly. "And that is all any of you have ever seen. I am a prize to be flaunted, no more! But no one has ever bothered to discover whether the prize is a hollow sham."

He frowned and lost any tendency toward amusement. "What is this nonsense? Do you think to disappoint me, lass? I promise you could never do that. Enrage, infuriate, and drive me to distraction, yes. But disappoint me—never."

"You can't know that," she almost whispered.

"Can't I?" Amusement had returned, and something far stronger. He raised his hand and allowed it to slide deliberately down to her beautiful white shoulders, left bare by the lace neck of her gown. "You are wrong to say you are not like other woman, lass. You are far more like them than you know. And you feel all woman at the moment. Shall I prove it?"

"That . . . It doesn't . . . It means nothing," she cried scornfully.

He laughed deeply. "Does it not? Did you find lovemaking with Lavisse satisfactory? No, don't bother to bridle and look daggers at me. Did you think I wouldn't guess? I knew because it has been the same with me. Or do you imagine I have been able to touch another woman since that day of the hunt?''

She trembled deeply under his touch. ''That will go away. It must!'' she whispered almost desperately.

His smile grew. ''I wish I might be so confident. Are you afraid of me, lass?''

''Yes! No! Oh, damn you! Don't you see? I thought marriage would be an escape, but it's an even greater trap. And I vowed that I would *never* give anyone power over me again. Never!''

His heart leapt within him at her words, and he knew an exultation he was careful to hide. ''Certainly not a husband. That would be too hopelessly middle-class,'' he agreed in amusement. ''But then, if we are being honest—and we have seldom been that with each other, I fear, lass—I swore I would never give you such power over me. Why do you think I stayed away so long, and work myself to exhaustion every day, so that I might sleep? I thought I could bring you here and remain unmoved, but I was wrong. I am the one in need of pity, for I had not even your drops to sustain me.''

She still trembled, but her eyes had half-closed under his hand on her shoulder. ''I tell you this is not love but madness,'' she moaned. ''We will both come to regret it.''

''Aye, perhaps you're right. But I have been mad since the first day I saw you. Did you doubt it? Open your eyes, lass. If we are both of us to be consumed, at least we will go willingly to our fate.''

Slowly she opened her eyes and watched, as if drugged by the drops she had sworn not to take, as his dark head lowered to her own. For a moment longer she resisted, and her last words before he took her mouth were, ''Damn you! Oh, damn you!''

It was not a gentle wooing. He had meant to go easy with her, particularly after his last roughness so long ago. But he should have known she would be as unpredictable in that as in all else. From the moment their lips met she seemed to abandon all control. She shuddered as if his touch were something she had long been in need of, and opened her mouth to his like a flower.

His passion flamed instantly at her response, and threatened all his good intentions. He crushed her to him, as starved as she for the taste of her. It had been too long . . . too long . . . and rightly or wrongly, the long torture of his self-imposed restraint was clearly at an end.

He had not meant this to happen, and deep within, some saner part of him knew it was a mistake, as she said. But it had indeed been inevitable from the first, and he had known when he first entered her bedchamber and found her crying like a bairn roused from a bad dream that he would not be able to leave her again that night.

He was undoubtedly a fool—a weakling and a fool. She had said it was not love but madness, and perhaps she was right. And though she had undoubtedly changed a good deal in the last weeks, and surprised him by her ability to settle into the difficult life he had brought her to, he was a fool indeed if he imagined anything was different between them. She had told him so herself just a moment ago. And if lately he had begun to hope that he had not been so mistaken in her after all, he was not fool enough yet to believe he had won his desperate wager with himself. And this would but give her a hold over him he had sworn never to give her.

Aye, he was indeed a fool. But even as he thought the words, he followed her down to the soft feather mattress beneath her, powerless to resist the spell she wove. His last conscious thought was to wonder that he had been able to resist her for so long.

21

Lady Sinclair was alone in the breakfast room the next morning when her new sister-in-law came in hurriedly, and with none of her usual grace.

She looked heavy-eyed, as if she had not slept well, and would seem to have dressed in a hurry. She looked quickly around the room and demanded abruptly, in her attractive husky voice, "GlenRoss? Have I missed him?"

GlenRoss's sister did not miss certain telltale signs that aroused all of her woman's curiosity, but she said calmly, "Yes, he is already gone, I fear."

Drewe's beautiful mouth drooped. "Oh, the devil! I must have overslept. Did he say when he expected to be back?"

Lady Sinclair looked puzzled. "Not for several days. At least that is what I understood. Didn't you know?"

Drewe stiffened, and there was a moment when her fascinated companion feared she would either throw something or burst into tears. Of the two, she looked far more capable of the former. "I see," she said ironically. "I am grateful to you for the information. Damn him to hell and back again!"

She then seemed to realize she was behaving badly, for she added impatiently, "I beg your pardon. It is just that I particularly wanted to speak to him about . . . something. If my language offends you, I'm sorry."

Lady Sinclair, who had long since realized that something

was very amiss in her brother's hasty marriage, said cordially, "Pray don't guard your tongue on my account, my dear. I frequently long to swear myself."

"The difference being that you are no doubt able to restrain your unruly tongue. But GlenRoss will have told you that my upbringing was of the worst, so I make my apologies."

"Well, no. He told me very little, in fact. Did you think we had engaged in a comfortable gossip about you after you left us last night? Quite the reverse was true. I admit I would have loved to, for I know very little about you, after all. But you must know by now that GlenRoss is among the most annoying of brothers, however dearly I love him. Are your brothers the same? I understand you have two. Do they go all moral and upright on you just when you are longing for a pleasurable bit of scandalmongering?"

Lady Drewe, who had seemed of two minds whether to remain or not, gave an unamused laugh and sat down at the breakfast table. "No, no, only coffee for me, thank you. I am not hungry. My brothers and I share very little except a mutual dislike, I'm afraid."

"Oh. I am sorry to hear that, for I can't imagine life without my own dear brothers, even though I am married now, of course. I am sure I dote on my dear James, but husbands are never the same as brothers, you know," she added frankly.

"That, at least, is inarguable," Drewe said in her abrupt way. "I believe you also have two?"

A shadow seemed to cross Lady Sinclair's usually cheerful countenance. "Now I do, though I can never seem to get used to the fact. I am very fond of both Ian and Robbie, of course, but poor Simon's death struck us all hard, you know. He was the nearest to me in age, and so we were particularly close. I have young Sim, who's staying with me just now. But it's not the same."

Drewe was regarding her with her straight, somewhat disconcerting stare. "How did he die?" she asked. "GlenRoss does not speak of him."

Lady Sinclair sighed. "He wouldn't, of course, for he was also very broken up over his death. You must have seen by now that he takes his responsibilities far too seriously, and I think he has always half-blamed himself. It was not his fault, of course, for Simon had indulged himself for far too long with tales of Scotland's past glories, and our injustices suffered at the hands of the iniquitous English. It is a common Scots fault, I fear, but in Ian such tales only seemed to make him the more determined to shoulder his responsibilities to the clan. In Simon they were far more disastrous. They bred a hatred for the English that was bound to end in tragedy, I suppose."

"What happened?" Drewe demanded rather harshly.

"To this day, no one quite knows, though we have our suspicions, of course. He was at university in Edinburgh, and in the wild way young men have of talking, especially in their cups, no doubt, was stirring up rather too much resentment again. That part I can well believe. But he was found brutally murdered one night. The authorities blamed it on a band of young Mohocks, which unfortunately are not limited to your country, I fear. But I have always had my doubts."

"In short, you believe he was murdered by the English!" Drewe said still more harshly. "My God, it wanted only that!"

Lady Sinclair regarded her curiously. "Had you heard none of this? It is just like men to keep such secrets. In fact, I'm not at all sorry I told you, for you must not be thinking, you know, that any of us hold it against all the English. There was a time, I'll admit, that I feared Ian did, for he took the death very hard, as I say. He blamed himself for not having sent Simon abroad, as he had himself been, and for not having scotched his wild talk, knowing it could be dangerous. But both ideas are ridiculous. And the very fact he could have married you, my dear, shows that he has at last gotten over it. In fact, I was wholly astonished when I received his letter saying he had married an Englishwoman, for it was the last thing I would have expected him to do."

"Or he of himself, for that matter! Oh God, I begin to think I must have been mad. As mad as he was himself! Did he tell you he offered for me out of pity?" Drewe demanded abruptly. "He did, you know."

"Good God. Having seen you, I cannot believe that, my dear. We have even heard of the great Lady Drewe Carlisle in our benighted part of the world."

Drewe laughed without humor. "Then you must know that I have at last made London too hot to hold me. I can only think I must still have been existing in shock. Or a fool's paradise! Only after last night . . . " Then she gave a harsh laugh. "But that was the most absurd dream of all, it seems. In the clear light of morning we are both sane again, as I predicted. Oh, God . . ."

She seemed to have forgotten her audience, for she was talking almost wildly, as if to herself. Lady Sinclair regarded her with a curiosity not untinged with pity. She had not come expecting to like her beautiful and notorious new sister-in-law, for as she had said, news of her exploits had indeed reached even Edinburgh. But she was a kindly woman, and could not see Drewe so clearly unhappy without being a little affected.

She hesitated, then said frankly, "My dear, the first months of marriage are always the hardest, I assure you. You are both so unsure of yourselves, and, after the first fine rapture wears off, beginning to chafe at the constraints of the wedded state. Forgive me, but you are, I think, put out because

GlenRoss forgot to tell you he would be absent for a few days. But that is just like a husband, for they always have other, more important things on their minds. They quite mean to tell you, but it somehow slips their minds. If I have suffered it one time I have suffered it a dozen, and it never even does to tax them with it, for ten to one they would swear they *did* tell you and firmly believe it themselves.''

Drewe did not even smile perfunctorily at this mild jest. "No doubt, but ours is hardly a typical marriage. He never wished to marry me, you see," she said impatiently.

"My dear, no man wishes to marry until he finds the ring on his finger. If is one of the wisdoms of the ages. And as for you to say such a thing, forgive me, but I have never heard anything so ridiculous. Don't try to tell me you didn't have any number of besotted fools dangling after you, for I wouldn't believe it. And whatever they say, men are but primitive creatures at heart. They like nothing better than to snag a prize others are lusting after. I doubt my noble brother is any exception.''

Drewe did laugh at that, though it sounded suspiciously like a sob. "Fools is right! They were none of them together worth so much as GlenRoss. But I always knew that our ways of life were too different. And you have but given me yet another reason for our marriage not to work. I was a fool to think it could be any different.''

"My dear, it is none of my business, I know, but you are very mistaken. I will confess I wondered at the marriage myself. Forgive me, but you have the reputation of being spoilt and pleasure-loving. But the transformation you have achieved here proves us all wrong. I was astonished when I heard GlenRoss had brought you to Lochabar, for because of who you are, it seemed rash beyond belief. You must know my sisters and I dislike the place, and even my mother would seldom set foot in it in the winter. I would not have been surprised if you had not lasted a week under its inconveniences. But you have lasted far longer than that, and even managed to make it more comfortable than I would ever have believed possible. And I know, for I am a housewife myself, that it must have taken you weeks of hard labor.''

Then she faltered a little at the look in her beautiful sister-in-law's eyes. ''What are you saying?'' Drewe inquired levelly after a moment. ''That GlenRoss has other houses he might have brought me to?''

Lady Sinclair was suddenly uneasy, but she could not refuse so direct a question. ''My dear, yes, of course, GlenRoss itself is but two hours from here, and though some think it too big, it is where we grew up, for it is much newer and far more comfortable. And then, of course, there are the house in Edinburgh and the manor at Stornmouth.''

''How many houses does he own?'' Drewe demanded, a little harshly.

Lady Sinclair was beginning to realize she had somehow said something she shouldn't. ''Well, five, counting the old house on one of the closes in Edinburgh, but it is so uncomfortable no one ever stays there. And of course the hotel in Paris, but that was bought years and years ago, and though it has undoubtedly increased in value, with the uncertain times in France at the moment, it hardly counts.'' She realized that with every word she was making things somehow worse, but didn't seem able to stop. ''My dear, what is it?'' she demanded at last.

''Why, nothing. Except that your brother clearly brought me here as a method of driving me back to London. He thought, like you, that I would not last a week, and no doubt counted on that fact. How ungenerous it was of me to destroy all his plans. But that can be remedied, of course.''

Lady Sinclair, regarding her beautiful sister-in-law in something like awe, could suddenly believe most of the stories she had heard about her. She looked magnificent, but about as human or approachable as a marble statue. But she had to try to do something to repair the damage she had unwittingly caused, and so said helplessly, "My dear, I'm sure you're mistaken. Good God, don't you know by now that Ian is chivalrous to a fault? Let any pitiful creature approach him with a tale of woe, and he is lost. He would never serve you such a turn."

"Wouldn't he?" Drewe was smiling, though it was not a pleasant smile, and she was very pale underneath. "You but confirm my own belief. I was the pitiful creature with a tale of woe. But he is less chivalrous than you believe, for he quickly saw he had gone too far this time and set out to undo the damage his too-ready chivalry had caused. Nor do I have any intention of disappointing him. I have also seen how disastrous such a union was for both of us, and will proceed with all speed to relieve him of such an irksome encumbrance."

She was gone from the room before Lady Sinclair could find her tongue or think of anything at all to say.

It was five interminable days later before GlenRoss returned home, and then it was late and he was tired and muddy from a hard ride.

He was on his way upstairs when a sound in his wife's sitting room drew him. He knew he would be late for dinner if he didn't go immediately to change, but there was a light in his eyes he could not quite manage to disguise, and he went in with a hasty step.

He found only his sister there, turning the pages of a periodical. The eager light faded, and he was aware of a sense of disappointment completely disproportionate to the event.

But he made himself say calmly, "What—are you still here, Lillibet? Where's Drewe?"

His sister looked up quickly and almost shrieked at sight of him. "Ian! Thank God you've come! Yes, I'm still here. A pretty thing it would be had I disappeared as well. Where on earth have you been?"

He came on into the room and poured himself a glass of whiskey. "At GlenRoss on business, as I told you. Where's Drewe?" he repeated again more sharply.

She did not answer his question, but said abruptly, "Why did you marry her, Ian?"

GlenRoss frowned and tossed down the whiskey. "Leave well enough alone, Lillibet!" he said impatiently.

"Aye, but *is* it well enough? She is English, and notorious, and spoilt, and I would have said none of those were for you. But I ended up liking her better than I expected to. So I repeat, why did you wed her?"

He turned away. "I said to leave it! I'll not discuss my marriage, even with you."

"And I think I should have insisted upon this conversation long before. She said it was out of pity. Was that . . . *can* that be the truth?"

He turned back quickly. "She said . . . ? Good God, don't tell me you discussed it with her?"

"No, she is as impossible as you," she said frankly. "Then tell me this. Why on earth did you bring her here, of all places?"

He turned away again. "Have done, Lillibet. You cannot help the situation by meddling."

She could almost have stamped her feet in vexation. "I begin to think it's time someone did! Was it to test her, Ian, or to drive her away?" she demanded bluntly.

He looked thunderstruck. "Drive her away? Who the devil put that into your mind?"

"She did, you fool. But I should have known it was to test her. Of all the idiotic, half-sprung, stupid ideas! But it is just like a man!"

"I . . . All right, yes, have it your way," he said after a moment. "But if you have been discussing it with her, you must know why. I offered for her out of pity, and against my better judgment, but I feared it would never last. Good God, what had I to offer her compared with the life she was used to? Our lives, our expectations—everything was different. She is used to constant amusement and flattery. I had nothing but hard work and a bleak landscape to offer her."

"And yet she accepted you," his sister pointed out dryly.

"Yes, she accepted me. But she had been . . . chastened, and I knew that mood was unlikely to last. In fact she is in the habit of leaping headlong into one disastrous scrape after another, and then running away from the consequences of her actions. I could not help fearing our marriage would be but another in the pattern."

"So you brought her here?" said his sister, not knowing whether to laugh or cry.

He shrugged again. "I had a wish to know if our marriage stood any sort of chance of succeeding. I was a refuge, but I feared that when she came to her senses, she would quickly regret her bargain. And I was fighting as well the general English perception that all Scots are little better than barbarians. It seemed to me she had best learn the worst at once. So I brought her here, as you say. I preferred to find out whether she could—or would—adapt herself to my way of life before it was too late for either of us."

"Oh, my dear," she said softly. "You love her very much, don't you?"

Something in her voice at last got through to him. He lifted his head and demanded sharply, "What is all this about? Where is Drewe?"

"Oh, my dear!" she said again tragically. "I am very afraid she has left you. And it is all my fault."

For a moment he was rigid under her hand. Then he gave a short, sharp laugh. "It would seem I have my answer," he said, and went and poured himself another glass of whiskey.

His sister regarded him in frustration. "Aren't you even going to ask why?"

"It little matters. I must presume you let slip, in your usual harum-scarum ways, that this was not my only residence. But you need not fear you drove her away. If she left because of that, it was but an excuse, believe me."

"Good God, I swear I could shake the pair of you! Tell me, did you ever give her any reason to stay? Did you ever make love to her?"

He gave the ghost of a bitter laugh. "Once—why do you think I fled so hastily?"

"I think that for a sensible man you are remarkably foolish," she scolded him roundly. "You said yourself she was used to constant amusement and attention. And yet you could find nothing better to do than to hold her at a distance. Here you have a beautiful, desirable wife, and you ignore her. Pray why should she stay?"

"You don't understand," he said impatiently. "My only novelty to her was that I didn't seem to fall at her feet as the other poor fools she was used to taking so much for granted and despised."

"What you mean is that you were a man and not a painted puppy! I would never have thought you could be such a fool. Why else do you think she married you? More, it seems to me she passed your absurd test with flying colors, for she not only remained here uncomplainingly but also made it far more comfortable than I would ever have believed it,'' his sister said strongly.

He was staring down into the fire with a harsh expression on his usually pleasant face, but now he said shortly, "For her own comfort! Not for me."

"I declare you're hopeless! Believe me, no woman puts herself to so much trouble for her own comfort. I begin to think you deserve to lose her."

"I have lost her," he said bleakly. He gave a harsh laugh again. "Or rather, I never had her. It was all but an illusion from the beginning."

"She said much the same, but I wish to hear no more talk of illusions! Confess, you mishandled her from the beginning, which is not a thing I would have expected of so excellent a whip! So now what do you mean to do? Let her return to London and divorce you?"

He shrugged. "Am I to drag her back against her will? You speak of the test as if it were inhuman, but this place is only slightly more inconvenient than my other homes. She is used to constant gaiety and distraction, I tell you. I have nothing to offer but hard work and relative poverty. I am richer than I let her believe, yes, but the bulk of my fortune is committed to my work, you know that. And not even for her will I abandon that. I can't. I knew from the beginning that it would never work. I only foolishly allowed myself to hope—"

"And yet she would not go to Edinburgh with me," Lady Sinclair reminded him meaningfully.

He frowned, considering it, but then shook his head. "I will confess I permitted myself to hope, when she seemed to fit in here better than I expected. That is why I allowed myself to . . . But never mind." Abruptly he turned to his sister. "I think you didn't like her, but I tell you her heart is in the right place. She is spoilt, yes, and careless of others. But I have known almost from the first that there was more to her than meets the eye. She has courage and spirit—more than any other woman I've ever known. She did work hard here, and without complaint. And she accepted every inconvenience without whining, even though she was used to a very different way of life. She comes from the worst possible background, despite her noble birth, for her brothers and that father of hers have never used her as they ought, or even looked after her as one would expect of any gently born girl. In fact she says she knows nothing of love, and I sometimes suspect it's true.''

"Yes, she said something of that," his sister admitted. "But feeling the way you obviously do about her, can you really let her go?"

"What else can I do? Drag her back by the hair? Demand that she love me? I foolishly thought that if I had her, I could teach her to in the end. But the truth is, she has no wish to give any man such control over her. I think she means it.''

"So you mean to allow her to disappear from your life? You are magnanimous. But have you thought that she might even now be carrying your child?'' demanded his sister deliberately.

His eyes flared to life and he instantly came back to take her shoulders in a hard grip. "Did she tell you that? Answer me, damn you!''

She seemed not to mind his mistreatment of her. "No, but you must admit it is at least a possibility. Will you allow it to be brought up in England, among all those painted fops, as you call them?''

"No, by God!'' He let her go and took a hasty turn about the room. "It might be true—and if I know her, she would never even tell me.'' He turned again toward his sister and barked out, "How long ago did she leave? Quickly, for there is not a moment to be wasted!"

She was pleased with the result of her stratagems, but a little startled that he seemed to mean to start out immediately. "Five days ago, but surely you will wait till morning to set out, Ian? I doubt she will make very good time, for she will hardly care to travel on the mail, and it is not easy to hire a post chaise to go all the way to London, even in Edinburgh. You should easily be able to overtake her before she reaches home again."

"I intend to overtake her long before that!" he said shortly. "She is my wife—and it is long past time she was made to acknowledge it!"

He was gone on the words, leaving his sister to stare after him in some bemusement. "And I'll wager that if he shows her that face, and sweeps her willy-nilly off her feet, not even the spoilt and much-sought-after Lady Drewe Carlisle will be able to resist him," she murmured to the empty room, and went to pack her bags. It seemed more than likely she would not be needed when the couple returned.

22

Drewe found the return journey from Scotland even more uncomfortable than her coming had been.

She had spent two interminable days in Edinburgh trying to arrange for the hire of a post chaise to take her to London, and by the time she at last set out, it was with the devout wish she might never set foot in Edinburgh again. But even more depressing had been the thought that in all likelihood her wish would be realized.

The journey south was a nightmare. The job horses were sluggards, the inns that enjoyed her distinguished patronage wholly unaware of the favor she conferred upon them, and this time there was no good-natured GlenRoss to ease her passage or tease her out of her sullens. Days of being shut up in an airless and badly sprung coach, with nothing to occupy her but her own unpleasant thoughts, did nothing to improve her temper.

On the fourth day out of Edinburgh, she was putting up at a posting house very near the border. The thought of returning to safe and familiar England was the only thing that had sustained her thus far; but curiously, her proximity to the border did not fill her with the unmitigated relief she had expected to feel. She had lacked even the energy to react with her usual temper to the fact that the bedchamber allotted to her overlooked the busy yard and that the fireplace undoubtedly smoked.

She was sitting in that chamber now, her chin propped on her hands, unaware of the occasional belch of smoke that issued forth into the room. She had been right that she would get very little sleep, for there were latecomers arriving even at that hour, and she had no doubt that long before dawn the noise would start up again, for the landlord had informed her that the mail coach would be setting out at four the next morning.

It little mattered, for she had not been sleeping anyway. She might have reverted to her drops, now that GlenRoss was out of the picture; but curiously enough, she had too much pride even now to go back on her word. It was absurd, for GlenRoss clearly no longer cared what she did. But she found she was no longer even tempted.

She had run through a gamut of emotions by then. Fury had been first and foremost, and had sustained her for several weary days. A pretty thing indeed when a mere Scottish bumpkin should have had the effrontery to grow tired of her. He had obviously wanted nothing from the first but her money for his precious schemes. Having obtained that, he probably intended to discard her as soon as he decently might.

Well, good riddance to him! When she thought of the discomforts she had endured, and the primitive nature of the home offered to her, all suffered uncomplainingly, it was a wonder she had lasted so long. To learn it was all for a jest was to drive her to a rage greater than she had ever known before. Oh, he had tricked her finely, and made a complete fool of her, and she should be glad enough never to see him again. Her only regret was that she had come away before telling him exactly what she thought of him.

That mood had made the rigors of the journey at least tolerable. But unfortunately it had all too soon deserted her and she felt nothing now but a profound and bitter depression.

It did not help that she was returning home to an even worse scandal than she had left. It was too much to hope that her own world would not take smug delight in the failure of a marriage they had all predicted was doomed from the beginning. Harry would also be impossible on the subject, of course, and was likely even to demand his forfeit back. In short, she had jumped from the frying pan into the fire by so hasty and ill-advised a marriage, and she was the last person to relish being forced to publicly acknowledge the fact.

Until her acquaintance with GlenRoss she had not been much given to self-examination, but when she considered the matter dispassionately, she was obliged to confess that she had no one to blame but herself. Her own conduct had been inexcusable from the first. She had deliberately tried to make him fall in love with her, for no other reason than that he had dared to scorn her and look at her with dislike. When he had had the good sense to continue to hold her at a distance, she had seen his indifference as a direct challenge, and had gone so far as to contract an odious wager with her brother—hardly the work of an innocent damsel!—that she could get a proposal out of him, despite his obvious dislike.

Well, she had succeeded, and perhaps it would teach her a much-needed lesson. It was undoubtedly poetic justice that she should have been the one to be spurned, for once. God knew she had seldom concerned herself with the feelings of those she had discarded because they bored her or had become too importunate. She had merely been annoyed when they refused to take their dismissal in good part.

From the realization of her own culpability in the whole tragicomic affair, it was inevitably but a short step to acknowledging ruefully that she had no real desire to return to London. For most of the length of her marriage that had been the only thought sustaining her, so that she hardly knew when it had begun to change. She had found a certain satisfaction in putting GlenRoss's house in order, of course, and in being useful for once. But there was more to it than that. She had gradually come to believe in what he was doing, and to care what happened to his people. She, who could scarce recognize her father's own tenants, and had never concerned herself with the fate of the less fortunate in her life, had had her eyes opened at last, and what she had seen had shocked her.

In fact, she realized that whatever the outcome, she had no intention of demanding her dowry back. It would be put to far better use in GlenRoss's hands than in satisfying her whims, and perhaps something good might arise out of this whole unpleasant mess.

She laughed a little bitterly at the thought of her brothers' faces when she told them. They would think she had gone mad, and perhaps she had. They would certainly believe her mad if they ever discovered that the thought of returning to London, and her old, pointless way of life, was becoming more and more unwelcome the closer she got. But the truth was, she had changed, somehow, and she doubted now if she would ever be the same again.

And GlenRoss? She had, until now, shied away from thinking of him, except to rail against him in her first white-hot anger. But knowing she would not sleep, and that she would be leaving Scotland tomorrow, no doubt forever, forced his image before her, no matter how much she resisted.

He had enraged, infuriated, puzzled, and even intrigued her. But alone among all the men she knew, he had never bored her. He had from the first piqued her vanity by palpably failing to fall at her feet as most other men did. He had countered her every move, had had the audacity to laugh at her, and had tumbled her ruthlessly from her pedestal.

That being the case, it was a mystery why, while he remained totally immune to her charms, she had committed the supreme folly of falling in love with him. It was no doubt ironic indeed. Nor did she know exactly when it had happened; but she suspected it had been far sooner than she cared to admit. The only sop left to her pride was the devout hope that he had never discovered the truth, for that would be unendurable.

As for GlenRoss, he had been carelessly kind, even attentive on occasion. He even—as she had very good reason to know—desired her. But he had plainly never been at any risk of losing his heart. Why should he? He had no use for the things other men prized in her: her beauty and outrageous caprice. He had despised her from the beginning, and she could not flatter herself she had ever given him any reason to change his opinion of her.

But then, what had she expected? she asked herself cynically. A fairy-tale ending? GlenRoss to discover that despite her selfishness and spoilt temper, her reputation and caprice, he could not live without her and come full tilt after her? That made her mouth twist with bitter mockery, for she had never even seen him angry. The thought of himself as romantic hero would no doubt have amused him greatly. The most she could hope for, when he discovered she was gone, was that he would shrug and go on about his life. She could not even flatter herself she had made a single dent in that life; and that was the most galling thing of all.

The thought that she would never again see his oddly attractive smile or hear him call her "lass" again cost her an odd pang. But she knew she had no one to blame but herself. She was proud and selfish, spoilt and spendthrift. She had never cared for anyone but herself in her whole life, and scarcely knew how to begin at this late date. She was not even a good wife, for all she knew how to do was to look beautiful and behave outrageously.

Worse, she thought she loved him now, but in truth she feared sometimes that that rumor was true: she possessed no heart. How could she expect to know how to love, when she had herself never known it, or been admired for anything but superficial qualities, not even by her father or brothers? She was a pitiful creature indeed, despite her birth and wealth, and that was the most lowering thought of all. That she should be brought so low at last might amuse GlenRoss very much, but unfortunately it changed nothing.

Well, he had taken the only thing he truly desired from her—her money—and was welcome to it. Let him do some good with it, for it was certain she would only waste it, as she had wasted everything else in her life. And the future? A polite divorce, no doubt, bringing about even more notoriety. And then what? She could not see, but a second marriage seemed out of the question. She had willfully thrown away the only chance she had ever had for happiness.

Her mouth and eyes were bitter as she stared into the fire, scarcely aware of the lateness of the hour. Mercifully the yard had grown quiet at last, and she supposed she should at least try to get some rest. It seemed scarcely worth the effort of rising and undressing, however, for she doubted she would sleep.

It was then, in the quiet house, that she heard the quick, firm step outside her door. There was the briefest of knocks, and to her surprise the door was thrust open without warning.

Even as she rose hurriedly, in mixed alarm and annoyance, for it was indeed very late and she had been a fool not to lock her door, she saw who was there. She was so astonished she sank down again bonelessly into her seat, for once beyond speech.

For it was GlenRoss who stood there, but a GlenRoss she had never seen before. He looked tired and dirty, his boots liberally splashed with mud from the bad roads, and still in his greatcoat, his whip in his hand. But it was more than that. Gone was the good nature, seemingly so ingrained, and the habitual twinkle in his very blue eyes. He looked, in fact, to be in a towering temper, and that surprised her so much she remained in her seat, even when he took one look at her, then thrust the door closed with one booted foot and came on into the room.

"So!" he said contemptuously, looking her up and down as if he had never seen her before. "I might have known you would take the first opportunity to cravenly bolt! That is, after all, the way you deal with all your problems, isn't it?"

She was so astonished she could only gape, for once beyond defending herself. He gave a harsh laugh and threw his whip onto a table, along with his hat and gloves. "What, speechless, my love? Or did you think I would not follow you? I should no doubt be happy that you condescended to remain with me for even those few months! It is no more than I expected, after all. You used me to escape the consequences of your own folly, and now that the hue and cry has no doubt died down, you escape from me as well. It was no doubt too much to expect even a word of apology or explanation from you."

She found her voice at last, her heart beating very fast. "If you think that, then why are you here?" she managed in a voice she scarcely recognized as her own.

He laughed again, without humor, and shrugged out of his greatcoat. "I scarcely know. To beat some sense into you? Believe me, I would if I could. To drag you back? I have been entertaining myself with visions of both, for days.

But your very surprise shows me exactly what opinion you have of me. The barbarous Scot, eh? I should no doubt meekly accept the divorce, content to have been given even these few months to worship at your altar. One should not hope for constancy or loyalty from the famous Lady Drewe Carlisle.''

"What are you saying?" she whispered.

"I am not surprised you don't understand, my dear. I have known from the first you possessed no heart. I hoped—but the more fool I, for everyone else knew the truth about you. You swore to bring me to my feet, did you not, and now that you have succeeded, you have no further use for me. I vowed, on the long ride here, to drag you back kicking and screaming if I had to, and finally teach you the lesson you so richly deserve. But now that I have found you, I doubt you are worth it,'' he said contemptuously, and turned away to the fire to hold his chilled hands out to it.

A strange, exultant feeling was growing within her. "You were never at my feet.'' Her eyes were on his harsh profile.

"I took good care not to let you know it, for I knew what would happen the moment I was fool enough to let you guess the truth. You have a habit of despising anyone who loves you, don't you, my sweet? You remained with me, and pretended such touching domesticity, only so long as I kept you guessing. I was far wiser when I was determined never to let you know the truth.''

"And that was?" she repeated very softly, becoming all the while surer of herself.

But he was in no mood to minister to her vanity. "I even brought you to Lochabar for precisely that reason, because I guessed I could not long hold you, and I was determined you should learn the worst from the beginning. I will admit you surprised me for a time. But of course, you would do anything to get your way, wouldn't you? And so long as I remained elusive, you could not be satisfied that you had made your conquest. How amused you must have been when I finally betrayed myself.''

She was watching him still, a smile beginning to play around her mouth. ''I was far from being amused,'' she said, still softly. ''Are you saying you took me to Lochabar as a test?''

He laughed again. ''It was the only sane thing I did in a series of foolish mistakes. I had vowed never to minister to your overweening vanity by offering for you, my sweet, however much I might be tempted. But then, when I found you heartbroken, so it seemed, I allowed my compassion to outweigh my reason. But I knew even then that such a change was unlikely to last, and that I had nothing to offer you but what you had despised from so many others.''

''And what was that?'' She was beginning to feel oddly breathless.

''Oh, no! You'll get no such satisfaction from me, you little termagant,'' he countered furiously. ''In truth, I don't know why I came, except to give you a piece of my mind. I flattered myself you were starting to change, and even learning to care for something besides your own precious self. But that's a laugh! I should have known it was impossible, for you're entirely heartless, aren't you, sweetheart? I should, in fact, have listened to what was said about you from the start, for it seems everyone else knew you better than I did myself.''

She had remained seated all this while, her eyes on his stormy face. But now she left her seat in a rush and launched herself upon him, all her pride abandoned. ''Oh, God! If I am heartless, it is because no one has ever taught me any better,'' she cried. ''I am selfish, spoilt—everything you said! But you could teach me better.''

He held her off by the wrists, his grip cruel. ''Only to have you leave me again when the mood suits you or you get bored? I think not. I need a wife and helpmate, not a spoilt heiress.''

"Good God, why do you think I married you?" she asked, laughing oddly. "You seemed to have . . . oh, everything I did not. A purpose in life, goals, and discipline. I meant to marry you long before that wretched affair with Haymont, for you were what I had been searching for all my life.''

"What are you saying?" he demanded, frowning.

"That my absurd wager with Harry was only to get an offer from you, not marry you. But I had long since made up my mind to marry you if I could overcome your dislike of me. I think now I must have been in love with you even then.''

Still he did not give in to her. "How do I know this is not but another of your damned tricks?''

She gave another reckless laugh that was half-sob. "You don't. But the truth is, I have discovered I cannot live without you. You were the only man who ever dared to stand up to me and show me what I really was. I vowed to get even with you, because I didn't in the least like what you showed me. But it is I who would seem to have been humbled, not you.''

A flame had leapt into his eyes, but still he did not surrender to it. "And what happens when this fit of humility ends and you realize I am no different from all the other fools who have loved you?" he demanded sternly.

She insisted upon the release of her wrists, and when he let them go put up her hands to pull his head down to hers. "The difference is, they admired only my beauty. You have resisted that from the beginning. If indeed you love me. I think you are the first person ever to really do so. And I hope it is because you see more in me than I see in myself. You are right that I have been heartless, but I am hoping you will be able to teach me how to love.''

He laughed oddly, and at last gave up the tight rein he had held on his control and swept her up in his arms. "I intend to—starting right now, lass," he said unevenly, and carried her to the bed, so invitingly near to hand.

A long time later, as they lay drowsy and contented, the fire, the only light in the room, casting its flickering shadows on the low ceiling, he said lazily, "This is all very well, but I must remind you that you said once you meant to give no man such power over you, lass. I must also warn you that I expect a conforming wife. One who will minister to my comfort and never argue with me. Who will be content to stand in my shadow and be meek and dutiful. She must, of course, wear the same gown years on end, and— "

She put her free hand over his mouth to stop him. "If you expected that, you would never have wedded me," she countered. "For my part, I expect someone who will dance attendance on my every whim and play the gallant on all occasions. You must, off course, shower me with jewels and presents, and never complain if I flirt with other men. It is, after all, the life I'm used to."

"Oh, I'll not complain, lass. I'll merely beat you." He grinned.

Drewe for some reason found nothing to complain of in this threat. After another long while he added ruefully, "Did you really think I meant to drive you away, lass? I must be a better actor than I thought."

She snuggled closer in his arms, but pretended indignation. "What else was I to think, when you tricked me so finely? When I think of the way you deceived me—"

"But I merely showed you what you half-expected anyway. I didn't even see you blink when I led you to your supposed future home, and you found it to be naught but a drafty castle on a frozen loch. Confess, you were convinced, like most English, that all Scots were little better than barbarians."

She sighed contentedly and dropped a kiss upon his bare chest. "Why else do you think I married you?" she inquired dulcetly. "But I must admit, until you came through that door this evening, I have been vastly disappointed in you. You were as tame and civilized as any Englishman, and I began to think the Scotsman's reputation was all nothing but a trick."

He turned her swiftly, and loomed over her, the fire once more in his eyes. "I see I shall have to bully you regularly. Or merely threaten to take you back to Lochabar, where conditions are as primitive as you could wish."

That reminded her of something, and this time it was she who held him away from her. "Do you really possess a number of other homes, all of them far more comfortable, you wretch?"

He grinned devilishly. "Oh, GlenRoss is too large to be comfortable, for my taste, but reared as you were, in the lap of luxury, you'll no doubt find it a vast improvement. The house in Edinburgh—the *old* house—is as inconvenient as you could wish, and makes even Lochabar look like a snug little place. I'd the intention of taking you there, but I feared my sister would spoil all. But the new house in Edinburgh I believe you'll find to your taste. We'll stop there on our way back."

He sobered. "But I want you to face the truth. I'm not in a class with your father, lass, for I've no great riches, and those I have are bespoken, so to speak. Even to keep you I'll not abandon my people. I hope you will find the life I can offer you comfortable enough, but there will be little room for the extravagances you're used to. No pledging your jewels at play, for I've far better use for the money; and no more outrageous escapades, for I fear you'll be too busy for that. Think it over carefully, for if you choose to come back to me, I'll not let you go again. You'll have no escape this time."

"I'd have thought I had already made my choice plain. But if you must have it in words, I think I adore you."

His reaction left her again breathless. But though the light in his eyes was almost overwhelmingly possessive, she held him off again. "Feeling as you did, why did you follow me?" she asked curiously.

"Why, to be sure, I did not mean to," he drawled, teasing her. "I had no wish for a reluctant wife, after all. But then my sister reminded me of the one thing that I could not ignore."

She frowned a little. "What on earth was that?'

"You might already be carrying my child," he said softly, watching her. "Had you thought of that?"

She flushed crimson, obviously startled, and her eyes flew to his. Then a slow smile began to play about her mouth. "I must confess I had not." She began to chuckle. "Lord, what an end to my career. I will never be able to live this down, I fear."

"Oh, you've no need to fear that, lass, for your fashionable days are clearly over," he told her wickedly. "Any woman so shameless as to be in love with her own husband has no claims to the world's attention. And by the time you are the mother of a brood of Highlanders you will have long since given up your desire to set the world on its ear. I don't doubt your devoted court will disown you completely when they learn the horrible truth."

She pulled him down to her and set about proving how little she cared.

ROMANTIC ENCOUNTERS